Ink or Swim

Catherine Dilts

Annie's®
AnniesFiction.com

Books in the Secrets of the Castleton Manor Library series

Library of Congress-in-Publication Data
Ink or Swim / by Catherine Dilts
p. cm.
I. Title
                    2018938861

AnniesFiction.com
(800) 282-6643
Secrets of the Castleton Manor Library™
Series Creator: Shari Lohner
Series Editor: Lorie Jones
Cover Illustrator: Jesse Reisch

10 11 12 13 14 | Printed in China | 9 8 7 6 5 4 3

Faith Newberry could almost imagine she had stepped back in time over 150 years as she entered Castleton Manor.

The spacious Great Hall Gallery had been transformed from a luxurious and refined setting to a scene of a rugged high seas adventure. Tall glass cases displayed whaling artifacts on loan from the Lighthouse Bay Whaling Museum. Paintings of ships and whales from the Jaxon family's art collection rested on large easels.

Vendors bustled around, preparing for the weeklong New England Whaling in History and Literature Conference, scheduled to begin the next morning. They draped tables in sailcloth and rough fishnet, providing a backdrop for every antique nautical item imaginable on this busy Thursday.

Faith saw enormous fishhooks, battered oars, oil lamps, sea chests, and even a ship's steering wheel composed of brass and wood. One vendor wore period attire consisting of a loose-fitting linen shirt and buckskin breeches. A brown mustache gave him the appearance of a walrus. Faith guessed this was for the benefit of the early guests who would be arriving that day.

As interesting as the antiques were, Faith didn't feel tempted to purchase anything until she noticed a bookseller. Faith loved the look, feel, and smell of books almost as much as she enjoyed the stories contained within their covers. Her job as the Castleton Manor librarian and archivist was a perfect fit. One of the many perks of working for the Jaxon family was being able to take Watson, her rescue cat, to work with her.

He mewed when Faith stopped.

"Impatient to begin the workday?" she asked him.

He blinked at her and twitched his stubby tail.

"Give me just a moment to check out these treasures."

Mysteries were her favorite, but Faith eyed the rows of books like a child staring through a candy store window. Historical accounts of New England whaling competed for space on the table with biographies of sea captains, travelers, and explorers. Fiction from modern regional authors vied with classic tales from the 1800s.

Faith was always on the lookout for special books to add to the impressive Castleton Manor library collection. Charlotte Jaxon and her son Wolfe owned many valuable first editions, but there was always room for one more.

Faith picked up a thick volume. The leather-bound copy of *Moby-Dick* on display was early but not a first edition. Likewise the copy of Louisa May Alcott's *Little Women*. Of course, an actual first edition would not have been sitting out where it could be damaged by careless shoppers. As an archivist, Faith knew to wear special gloves when handling precious books, but most people didn't. Still, it had been worth browsing.

"May I help you?" The vendor was a pleasant woman who wore her hair in a neat white bun. "We're not quite set up for sales yet, but I'll make an exception if an item has caught your eye."

Faith prepared to apologize for distracting the woman until she noticed a side comb inside a display case. Carved from a single piece of creamy alabaster material, the comb was decorated with a delicate pattern of twining roses. Faith could imagine how lovely it would be against her long chestnut hair. "Is that ivory?"

"Yes, and it's an antique," the vendor said. "The sale of ivory nowadays is regulated to make certain it wasn't harvested illegally."

"Do you mean poached?" Faith asked. "Like from endangered African elephants?"

A broad smile dimpled the woman's rosy cheeks. "You are well-informed. That's exactly the problem. I have a certificate dating this whale ivory to 1853. It's perfectly legal." She began to open the case. "Would you like to try it on?"

"It's beautiful, but I have to open the library." Faith waved a hand in the direction of the doors at the end of the gallery. The manor was not yet officially open for the conference, but a few guests had already checked in. "Besides, I doubt I could afford it."

"You might be surprised at how reasonably priced antiques can be," the vendor replied. "Just think about it."

Faith turned her focus to work as she strode to the library. The conference was scheduled to run a bit longer than most events held at the manor. In addition to her librarian duties, Faith was planning to give a talk about men's adventure novels versus the women's literature of the era. The conference started tomorrow, and she needed to ensure that everything was in order.

When Faith unlocked the door, she expected Watson to scoot past her.

"Watson? Now where did you go?"

The handsome tuxedo cat sat beneath a painting of a whaling ship. A sperm whale dived into the water, escaping the harpoon thrown from a wooden ship with huge white canvas sails. Watson seemed mesmerized.

"You must be imagining all the delicious tunaroons Midge could make out of that whale." Faith's veterinarian friend, Midge Foster, also owned Happy Tails Gourmet Bakery, where Faith bought Watson's favorite treats. Faith leaned down to lift Watson into her arms. "Or would those be whale-aroons?"

Faith opened the door and stepped into the incredible library. Red velvet chairs arranged in front of a massive fireplace encouraged guests to enjoy their favorite novel in sumptuous surroundings. There was plenty of reading material. Books filled the spacious two-story room.

Faith had just seated herself at her ornately carved antique desk when Wolfe Jaxon entered the room. As usual, he was impeccably dressed in a tailored suit. His thick dark hair, streaked lightly with gray, was neatly styled. Faith never ceased to go a little weak in the knees in the presence of her handsome boss. *He's my employer*, she chided herself.

Wolfe carried himself with the confidence of a man successfully managing his family's ancestral home. In 1895 Captain Angus Jaxon, a wealthy shipowner, had built Castleton Manor in Lighthouse Bay, Massachusetts. A decade ago, Wolfe's mother, Charlotte, had begun hosting literary events in the manor. They were an immediate hit. The mansion on Cape Cod was the ideal setting for booklovers' conferences, but hosting one with whaling-era literature as its focus seemed particularly suitable.

Watson walked over and rubbed against Wolfe's ankles.

"Good morning, Watson." Wolfe scratched behind the cat's ears.

When Wolfe turned his attention to Faith, Watson retreated to one of the chairs near the fireplace.

"Tonight's weather should be fine for the launching ceremony," Wolfe said. "The forecast calls for clear skies, and the temperature isn't supposed to dip below the forties."

The Jaxon family had contributed generously to building the whaling museum's replica whaling ship. Charlotte planned to christen the ship in a purely symbolic ceremony. The *Constance Merit* was not intended to sail away from the dock.

"That sounds chilly for an outdoor party," Faith said. "Although we have been enjoying unseasonably warm weather for November."

Wolfe seemed concerned. "We arranged for a canopy on deck and strategically placed patio heaters. I hope the night air won't be too uncomfortable for you."

Faith felt her cheeks flush. She hadn't meant to sound critical of her employer's plan. "I'll dress warmly and station myself close to a heater," she assured him.

"Terrific. I look forward to seeing you there." Wolfe had a dazzling smile, made more striking by his blue eyes. "Mother wanted our employees to get the first peek at the *Constance Merit* as a thank-you for all the hard work they do to make the literary events a success."

"It's a very generous invitation," Faith said. Only Castleton Manor employees, the museum curator and his staff, and Lighthouse Bay VIPs had been invited to the private party.

Wolfe glanced around the room. "It's obvious you've been busy. The library is certainly ready for a week of whaling lore."

Model ships, complete with ropes and sails, lined the fireplace mantel. Two sturdy glass display cases stood against a walnut-paneled wall.

"I've arranged your family's ship log in this case." Faith stood and walked around her desk. She pointed to one of the display cases. "Right in the middle of your scrimshaw collection."

Faith had positioned the worn, leather-bound log from Angus Jaxon's ship in the center of the case. She had opened the log to a page describing a stormy sea crossing. While the SS *Honoria* had not been a whaling ship, the log would still be of great interest to the historians attending the conference.

Scrimshaw aged to a golden hue surrounded the log. Scrimshaw was a decorative art form invented by American sailors. The subject matter was typically ships, whales, and mermaids carved into whalebone, ivory whale's teeth, or ivory walrus tusks.

Beside the log, she had set the Jaxon family's valuable copy of the Herman Melville novel about a great white whale.

The other display case contained Hawaiian historical and cultural items from the early 1800s. The items were brought by one of the guests, Tasi Kekoa. Faith had assisted her in arranging the artifacts in the case.

Just then, Tasi entered the library. The tall Polynesian woman greeted Faith and Wolfe and joined them at the display case. Tasi peered into the case. "Is that a first edition of *Moby-Dick*?"

"Yes," Wolfe said. "Castleton's library contains many first editions and other rare books."

And Faith was the collection curator. She felt blessed to have such a great job.

"Miss Kekoa has an impressive collection on display too," Faith said.

"Please call me Tasi." She stepped over to the other display. Her long dress, in a colorful print of tropical foliage and flowers, swirled around her ankles.

Faith and Wolfe studied the display of fishhooks, handwoven baskets, ancient fishnet, wooden bowls, shell jewelry, and faded black-and-white photographs of historical scenes from island life.

"They may not look like much," Tasi admitted, "but these are historical treasures I am grateful to have been able to preserve for study."

"I think the collection is wonderful," Faith said. "I can almost imagine what life on Hawaii was like back then."

"We are grateful for your contributions, and we'll do everything in our power to take good care of them," Wolfe told Tasi. "The cases are locked, and the library will also be locked when Faith is not present."

"Security hardly seems necessary," Tasi said. "Lighthouse Bay is such a pleasant little town. But I do appreciate your concern. These items are of immeasurable historical value."

A couple strode into the library. They were about the same height, but the man was on the heavy side and the woman was thin as a reed. She wore her silver hair in a neat bob. The man's gray locks were a wild tangle. He carried a briefcase with combination locks on each latch.

He approached the group and thrust out his free hand to Wolfe. "Raymond Prather. Here for the conference."

Wolfe shook Raymond's hand. "I'm glad you could make it, Mr. Prather."

"This is my wife, Judith," Raymond added.

She smiled and nodded.

A gray-haired woman carrying a cherrywood cane with a carved ivory handle entered the library. She stopped and leaned on the cane. "So this is where you disappeared to," she huffed.

"And this is my sister-in-law, Agnes VanStuth," Raymond said, sounding less than pleased about the introduction.

"I've read about you both," Tasi said to the Prathers. "You're famous for your amazing scrimshaw collection. May I ask if you brought the *Essex* piece?"

"Got it right here." Raymond tapped the side of the briefcase. "I'm not letting it out of my sight."

"That's a good idea," Tasi said. "The piece is a unique historic treasure."

"We would be happy to put it on display," Wolfe offered. "I can assure you that your scrimshaw will be safe in the manor."

Raymond shook his head. "I'm keeping it with me. Don't need any prying eyes as of yet."

"But you've brought it to the conference," Tasi protested. "Surely you'll present this exciting discovery to the rest of us. Perhaps during your talk?"

"It's going to Boston after the conference," Raymond said. "Not ready for display."

"Excuse me," Faith chimed in. "What is the *Essex*?"

While her husband was abrupt and unmannered, Judith seemed refined. She answered this time, her voice soft. "The jewel of my collection is scrimshaw from the whaling ship the *Essex*. The tragic true tale of this ship inspired Melville's *Moby-Dick*. As you can imagine, the scrimshaw is extremely valuable."

"We paid a pretty penny for this old piece of whale tooth." Raymond lifted the briefcase and gave it a shake. "Quite a feat. It's highly sought-after, you know. But we're the ones to catch it."

"What makes it so rare?" Faith asked.

"The *Essex* was a whaling ship that was rammed by a whale in 1820," Wolfe explained. "The ship sank, and the crew went through a harrowing struggle to survive. If any artifact is proven to have come from the *Essex*, it would be worth a fortune to historians and collectors."

"I would not have risked my life savings if I did not believe it was authentic," Judith said, her words crisp.

As another guest entered the library, Faith heard clicking claws on the hardwood floor, fading as the duo stepped onto the plush carpeting. The man was short and sturdy. He had boyish features, but Faith guessed he was close to Wolfe's age, perhaps in his midforties. He wore a beige cardigan over a white dress shirt, and his striped bow tie tilted at a slightly crooked angle.

A black-and-brown short-haired dachshund followed at his heels. The dog also wore a beige cardigan, tailored for its long torso. Fastened to its collar was a tiny matching bow tie.

The cat was intrigued by the new guest. The dog was horizontally blessed and vertically challenged with legs barely tall enough to keep his extraordinarily long midsection from dragging on the floor.

When the cat hopped off the chair, the dog backed behind his human's legs.

What a timid fellow, *the cat thought. He retreated a step and sat on the carpet to show the dog he meant him no harm.*

After a moment, the dog peeked past his human's legs at him. He smiled and wagged his tail, his long, pink tongue rolling past jagged doggy teeth.

The dog might be short, but his chest and legs were powerfully muscled. Better to have as a friend than an enemy, the cat decided.

And judging by that smile, he guessed they would be friends.

"Boomer, be nice to the kitty," the guest said. He glanced at Faith, a blush creeping across his cheeks. "My puppy's name is Captain Boomer. That's a character in *Moby-Dick*. My name is Milton Waldrin."

While Wolfe shook Milton's hand and made introductions to the other guests, Faith knelt and reached out a hand to the timid dachshund. "Hi, Boomer. I'm Faith."

The dog sniffed Faith's hand, then took a step from behind Milton. She gave him a gentle scratch behind the ears.

Watson inched closer. He and Boomer touched noses as they gave each other a thorough face sniffing.

"I'm very much looking forward to speaking at the conference," Milton said. "I'm a historian with a particular fondness for the whaling era." He zeroed in on Raymond's briefcase. "Is it in there? The *Essex* scrimshaw? May I see it?"

Raymond clutched the briefcase to his thick chest. "The *Essex* is not available for public pawing."

"Won't you show it to us?" Tasi wheedled. "Mr. Waldrin and I are both experts in the field of scrimshaw art. I understand your find is so new it hasn't even been authenticated yet. I would love to be one of the first to see it."

Raymond seemed about to launch into a loud and aggressive response.

But Judith placed a thin hand on his sleeve. "Perhaps later," she said to the others. "We've just arrived, and we need to get settled into our room. I'm exhausted from our drive." She headed toward the library door.

Raymond ignored his wife. Faith considered offering to accompany Judith to her room, but Agnes followed her sister.

"No show today," Raymond said. Then he finally seemed to notice Judith and Agnes waiting in the doorway. "I'll be leaving now."

"Just a peek?" Tasi clasped her hands together. "Seeing the *Essex* scrimshaw would be the highlight of the conference."

"No!" Raymond snapped. "We've arranged to have an expert in Boston assess the authenticity of the piece after the conference. Until then, there will be no viewing. Can't risk having some fool toss around inaccurate statements."

2

Raymond's rude words silenced everyone in the room.

Judith turned to glare at her husband. Faith saw Boomer crouch low to the floor, his tail tucked underneath his long body. The poor puppy was frightened by Raymond's angry voice. Watson flattened his ears against his head, a sure sign he was upset.

The steady ticking of the grandfather clock filled the room until Tasi responded. "I am recognized as an expert in the field of whaling-era art." She folded her arms across the front of her colorful dress. It was obvious from the tears at the corners of her brown eyes that Raymond's statement had offended and hurt her. "I would not authenticate the piece without going through a proper examination. I merely wanted a quick peek."

Faith expected Raymond to apologize for insulting Tasi, but his face darkened with anger.

"There could be no harm in showing the *Essex* scrimshaw to us," Milton said. "Until it is seen by your Boston expert, our opinions should not count, even if we entertain doubts."

Faith glimpsed a pained expression on Judith's face. The woman had said she spent her savings on the *Essex* scrimshaw. She would be financially devastated if it was a fake. It made Faith wonder why her husband refused to let two experts examine it now.

"What doubts?" Judith asked. "Do you know anything with certainty, or are you just spreading awful rumors?"

"The possibility of any articles surviving the demise of the *Essex* is remote," Milton said. "The ship sank. Any items belonging to the sailors who lived through the ordeal would surely have surfaced in a museum or a family collection long ago. I understand your concern that the *Essex* scrimshaw might not pass inspection."

Raymond's mouth dropped open. His untidy hair seemed to stand on end, and his face quivered with building rage until he erupted. "What are you trying to imply, you half-pint historian? Are you accusing us of deliberately harboring a fraud? The *Essex* scrimshaw is real!" He clutched the handle of the briefcase so tightly that his knuckles turned white, and he balled his free hand into a fist.

Milton raised his arms in front of his face.

Boomer whined.

Faith felt helpless. Should she step between the men and risk being dragged into their fight?

Instead, Wolfe held up his hands and smoothly took charge of the situation. "Mr. Prather, I'm certain Mr. Waldrin didn't mean to question your honesty. We are all excited by your discovery. You must understand how eager people are to see a piece of art with such an amazing historical background."

Wolfe's commanding tone seemed to calm everyone. Raymond took a deep breath and relaxed his grip on the briefcase handle. Milton lowered his arms.

Judith approached. "We have a lot invested in our little piece of ivory. Perhaps we take it a bit too seriously." She looped her arm through her husband's and gave a tug. "Come along, dear. Let's get settled into our room, shall we?"

Raymond glared at Milton.

The smaller man held out his trembling hand. "Let's not get off on the wrong foot," Milton said. "We'll be here all week in this beautiful mansion. I'd hate to spend it with a cloud of ill will hanging over us. I apologize for offending you."

Judith nudged Raymond with her elbow.

Raymond grudgingly shook Milton's hand. "Apology accepted."

As the trio left the library, Boomer sat up, his tail wagging.

Milton thanked Wolfe for defusing an ugly situation, then led his shy dachshund from the room.

"What a way to start a conference," Tasi said. "I'm glad the tension blew over so quickly."

"The rest of the week should be smooth sailing," Wolfe said.

As Faith watched the feuding guests work their way past the gallery vendors, she wished she could be as certain.

The rest of Faith's workday was spent in pleasant routine.

Finally, the last of the curious vendors and early guests left the library. Faith locked up and walked past garden beds snuggled under November blankets of mulch. Watson trotted along beside her until they neared home.

The old gardener's cottage was another perk Faith enjoyed as the Castleton Manor librarian and archivist. The stone exterior was sturdy enough to weather any storm, and recent renovations made for a bright and cheerful interior. It had a classic Cape Cod feel, down to small touches like scrimshaw pieces artfully arranged with seashells and bits of driftwood.

Watson bolted past Faith in a black-and-white streak, beating her to the door.

"You always have to be first," she observed. "But I don't see the point. You still have to wait for me to unlock the door."

He refused to respond.

After feeding Watson, Faith selected wool pants, comfortable boots that could accommodate warm socks, and a green cowl-necked sweater. With a jacket, she could endure the walk from the museum parking lot to the public dock where the *Constance Merit* was permanently docked.

Faith went "cat fishing" with Watson's feather-on-a-string toy. She tried to give him extra attention when she knew she'd be out for the evening.

She placed a tunaroon in his bowl. "It's not a whale-aroon, but I hope it'll do."

Watson began eating his treat with his usual delicacy.

"I promise I won't stay out too late. We have work tomorrow. The conference starts in the morning."

When Faith stepped outside, she thought Wolfe may have been overly optimistic to believe the weather forecast. The wind raced around the side of the cottage as she locked the door. The evening felt every bit like early November, with a chill in the air that hinted at snow.

Faith drove the short distance to the small town of Lighthouse Bay. Excitement about the museum's replica whaling ship had inspired shopkeepers to decorate their windows with even more nautical decor than usual. They were probably hoping to capture some souvenir dollars from the conference attendees. Their windows displayed whale-themed clothing, coffee mugs, lampshades, jewelry, plush toys, and paintings.

As Faith parked, she spotted her friend Brooke pulling up in her sporty red car. Brooke had recently been promoted from sous-chef to head chef at the manor. Faith knew the promotion was well deserved. Her friend was an incredible cook and an extremely hard worker.

Laura, the young housekeeper and Faith's occasional library helper, climbed out of the passenger side.

"I was going to ride in the manor van, but Brooke offered me a ride. Who could resist arriving at a party in a red sports car?" Laura was every bit the working college student in her bulky cable-knit sweater, plaid skirt, thick tights, and clogs. But she seemed to have forgotten her coat. She shivered and hopped up and down, making her blonde ponytail sway.

"I thought it was supposed to be warmer than this." Brooke wrapped her arms around herself. "That wind has a bite to it." Her boots were fashionable, with heels that clacked along the dock, but they didn't look warm. Neither did her knit dress. But at least she wore a coat.

"Wolfe said there would be a canopy and heaters on the deck," Faith said.

"Then let's hurry," Laura urged.

They headed down the well-lit street to the dock. White twinkling lights had been strung along the railings and twined up the lampposts.

As they walked, they caught up with two men and three women dressed in period costume.

"How fun," Laura said. "People from the museum dressed up for the party."

Lou Bennett, the museum curator, wore a walrus mustache like the vendor Faith had seen in the manor gallery. His whiskers must have been artificial, as Faith hadn't noticed them on him last week. Lou's vintage jacket had been a ship captain's. It had long tails and plenty of brass buttons.

The other man had a black beard, and he was dressed in the loose cotton shirt and tan slacks of a sailor. His outfit was topped with a jaunty hat, the ribbons flapping in the wind.

Two of the women wore long dresses typical of the early 1800s, the simple attire of a housewife or a shopkeeper, while the third woman wore a hoopskirt that might have been supported by an intricate frame of whalebone in days gone by. Hers was most likely made of modern materials, but her outfit didn't appear any easier to manage in the wind. She shrieked and laughed as she nearly took flight.

Lou came to her aid, and one of the women grabbed her other arm.

"The hoopskirt doesn't seem very practical," Laura remarked.

"They look warmer than us," Brooke said. "I could use a few more layers of clothing."

Faith, Brooke, and Laura rushed forward when the wind gusted. They reached the ship with other manor employees, city council members, the mayor of Lighthouse Bay, and Wolfe and Charlotte.

The group huddled together as the wind tossed heavy, wet

snowflakes that stuck to the side of the ship. The canvas sails were not yet attached to the three tall masts. The rigging would wait for spring when the weather would be less damaging.

"I'm glad you talked me into renting more heaters," Wolfe told his mother. "This snow was not in the forecast."

"It's a wise son who listens to his mother," Charlotte teased. Her dark hair was covered with a cream-colored cashmere scarf that matched her calf-length coat. "Let's get on with the dedication, shall we?"

The museum curator and the mayor both might have planned longer speeches, but the weather seemed to keep them succinct. A pastor led the group in an old-fashioned prayer for safety on the high seas. Then Charlotte said a few words and smashed a bottle of sparkling water against the bow.

Lou escorted the group up the permanent gangway, a wheelchair-accessible ramp with sturdy railings. The museum curator described every detail of the replica whaling ship.

Historically correct gear had been arranged as though the ship were about to head to sea to hunt whales. Even harpoons were on display, although Lou pointed out that they were not functional. It would be too dangerous with tourists and children on the ship to have working harpoons.

The cat waited until all the humans exited the van and quickly escaped before the last person closed the door. There was no way he was going to be left out of a party dedicating a ship that could capture a whale. His person thought she could lock him up in the cottage, but he had his ways.

He trotted down the dock, darting from shadow to shadow. No one seemed to notice as he worked his way onto the replica whaling ship. While the dock smelled faintly of fish and the sea, the ship itself lacked odors of interest to a cat. Freshly hewn wood and varnish gave no hint of the tasty treat he craved.

Then the humans emerged from the lower deck by going up a ladder and out a hatch.

The cat had seen enough. He didn't know what a whale smelled like, but he was certain there wasn't one anywhere near this ship.

He crept down the gangway, invisible to people more interested in the buffet table than a cat out for a nice ramble.

"I can't imagine sleeping in one of those tiny bunks for two or three years," Laura said. "There was no privacy."

"And it was dark below deck," Brooke added. "If whaling hadn't been made illegal to save endangered species, it might have died out for lack of people willing to hunt them."

"People still hunt whales," Lou said. "But obviously not in ships like this. Fortunately, some whale populations have made a comeback, but others are in danger of extinction. The museum is starting a program to raise money for whale conservation. Whales are still in need of protection."

"It's hard to believe, considering a whale was able to sink a ship this size," Wolfe said.

Lou nodded. "The *Essex*. That was one angry whale. And while that incident might be one of the most famous, it's by no means the only instance of whales sinking ships."

When the tour was over, people gathered in the bow of the ship to hear classic rock played by the local band Groaning Bones.

The bass player, Peter Foster, was Midge's husband. Tall and wiry, with neatly groomed sandy brown hair and glasses, Peter looked more like the accountant he was than a rock star.

Brooke and Laura joined Midge in folding chairs in front of the band. The canopy and the heaters offered shelter from the snow and warmth, but Faith didn't think the party would last much longer. A few people were already exiting the ship down the gangway.

Faith collected a small plate of goodies from the buffet table and leaned against the bulwark facing the small bay. It felt late, but according to her watch it was only seven thirty.

White-tipped waves pushed against the ship and the dock. The chilly air smelled mildly of brine and fish. A watery passageway between the *Constance Merit's* dock and the north dock was barely wide enough for the sailboats and yachts docking in Lighthouse Bay.

Faith watched the other dock through finely falling snowflakes. She tugged her coat closed, and she had just decided to head for the canopy when she glimpsed a cat on the far dock. It trotted along with purpose, as if it was late for an appointment, passing two men huddled in conversation.

Faith's eyes widened in surprise when she realized it was a black-and-white tuxedo cat with a stubbed tail. There was no chance there was a cat identical to Watson in the small town of Lighthouse Bay. She yelled his name, but between the guests' conversations, the band, and the wind, there was no way Watson could hear her.

How on earth did he get to town?

Faith briefly considered asking a friend to accompany her, but when she glanced under the canopy, Brooke, Midge, and Laura were singing along to a Beatles cover. They were having such a good time that Faith couldn't bear to disturb them. It would take her only a few minutes to grab Watson and return.

Faith stepped down the gangway and hurried down the dock. The walk was farther than she realized, and she was glad she wore comfortable boots.

The north dock was not geared toward tourists, and it lacked cheerful twinkling lights. A few boats bobbed against old tires cushioning the weathered wood. Most of the designated mooring spots were empty, the boats placed in storage for the winter.

Faith had lost sight of Watson, but maybe the two men could tell her which way he'd gone. She approached cautiously, only able to see their silhouettes as they slipped into the shadows between two stacks of crates. One was dressed in a utilitarian peacoat, and the other wore street clothes and a walrus mustache like the museum curator and the vendor at the manor.

The men seemed to be hiding, which made Faith nervous, but she was even more anxious to retrieve her wandering cat. Besides, the *Constance Merit* was close enough that she could yell for help. Faith tried not to dwell on the fact that her voice hadn't carried between the two docks only moments ago when she'd called out to Watson.

The wood dock had become slick under the thin layer of snow. Faith was beginning to consider the foolishness of her lone journey when she caught a glimpse of black-and-white fur. Watson was a resourceful cat, but spending a night outdoors in a snowstorm was not a situation Faith intended to allow. If she could catch him.

Watson sat on the end of the dock, staring out at the choppy waves.

Faith would have to pass the stack of crates surrounding the two men to reach the cat. As she neared the crates, a spear with a rope trailing it sliced through the veil of snowflakes.

Then a man cried out.

A scream caught in Faith's throat, terror reducing the sound to an alarmed squeak. Snow pelted the dock, blurring the scene.

The man with the walrus mustache emerged from between the crates, slipping and nearly falling. He vanished into the shadows.

Boots clomped across the dock. A figure bundled in a bulky, hooded coat approached the crates. A moment later, the person dragged the spear and rope across the dock.

Faith found her voice. She screamed.

3

Faith almost screamed again when a hooded figure ran toward her through the falling snow. Then she realized it was Officer Jan Rooney. The petite police officer's brown eyes peeked out from a black balaclava-style hood that covered her nose and hair.

"That was fast," Faith said. "I didn't even have time to dial 911."

Officer Rooney tugged the hood down around her neck, exposing her face to the cold. Snowflakes drifted onto her short black hair. "With the party on the ship tonight and more tourists in town than usual, the chief put extra officers on patrol. I noticed suspicious activity on this dock and was headed here to investigate. Your scream must have scared them off." She sounded disappointed that Faith had interrupted her surveillance.

"Only one of them," Faith replied. "The other might have been struck with—" She closed her eyes, picturing the object slicing through the falling snow. "A harpoon."

Officer Rooney raised one dark eyebrow. "A harpoon?"

"Two men were talking between those crates." Faith pointed at the stacks. "Then I saw a harpoon fly through the air. One man ran away. The other man might have been hit. Someone retrieved the harpoon and vanished over the side of the dock. We should see if the man between the crates needs help."

"Stay here," Officer Rooney ordered, then sprinted down the dock.

Faith followed but stayed several paces behind the police officer. As Rooney stepped between the crates, Faith noticed scattered fifty-dollar bills, boot prints in the fresh snow, a dark streak trailing toward the edge of the dock, and a receipt with the distinctive logo of The Fishwife's Attic antique shop. Faith had been involved in crime solving before, and she knew the clues could be important later. The boot prints would soon disappear under falling snow. Faith pulled out her cell phone and snapped several photos.

Officer Rooney spoke in police code into her walkie-talkie. The combination of words, letters, and numbers meant nothing to Faith. A raspy reply came back. Finally, Rooney emerged into the light.

"Is he okay?" Faith asked.

Officer Rooney held up her hand. "I told you to stay back there."

Faith wondered why the officer was not at the man's side, administering first aid. Maybe he hadn't been hit by the harpoon. "Watson is on this dock somewhere. I have to find him."

"Your cat?" Rooney asked. "Why didn't you leave him at home?"

"It's complicated," Faith said. *Watson is complicated. Whatever he's up to, he can't stay out tonight in this snow.* She shivered, wrapped her arms around herself, and stomped her boots on the dock in an attempt to keep her chilled blood circulating.

Police Chief Andy Garris called out orders as he marched down the dock. A former marine, the chief was tall and well-built. He never failed to command the attention of those around him.

Faith knew Chief Garris was a kind man at heart. Even so, she was nervous as she gave her statement to him, telling what little she had seen and offering to send him the photos she had taken. As she had expected, the boot prints were now buried under a layer of snow.

"I wish I could tell you more, but the man who ran away resembled half the men at the *Constance Merit* dedication. I didn't get a good look at whoever—" Her lips started to tremble as tears filled her eyes.

"So you didn't see which direction the object came from?" Chief Garris asked.

Faith pointed toward the dark smear. "It came from that way, but I didn't see the face of the person who threw it." A thought occurred to her, and she blurted out, "Why would the other man run away? He must have something to do with it. If he was innocent, he would have stayed to help."

"People often panic in these situations," Garris answered. "Let's table the question of guilt for now."

When Dr. Greco arrived, his bald head covered with a thick knit cap and his short frame wrapped in a bulky quilted coat, Faith's heart sank. Dr. Greco served as the local coroner. His presence meant bad news for the man between the crates.

Dr. Greco approached Chief Garris, and the two men walked into the shadows.

"May I make a phone call?" Faith asked Officer Rooney.

"Of course. You're not under arrest." Rooney tugged her hood back into place, muffling her words. Even so, Faith heard her mumble, "Not yet."

Faith called Brooke, hoping her friend's cell phone was on and audible above the band.

"Where are you?" Brooke asked. "We've been looking all over for you."

"On the north dock," Faith replied. "I was trying to find Watson."

"I see flashing lights," Brooke said. "What's going on?"

"I'm coming back to the ship."

"You wait right there. We'll come to you."

Faith ended the call. She blinked away the snowflakes melting on her eyelashes. They mingled with the tears building from anxiety about Watson and the realization that she had likely just witnessed a murder. *Where is that cat?*

"Watson!" Faith's voice was muffled by the falling snow.

"There he is." Officer Rooney pointed toward the end of the dock.

Watson stood under a dim light, the black parts of his tuxedo markings frosted with white flakes.

Faith started to run to her cat.

But Rooney held her arm. "No going past the crime scene," the officer said gruffly.

Watson scampered over to Faith, leaving a trail of tiny cat prints in the snow.

Faith scooped him up into her arms. "How did you get to town, Rumpy?" she asked him.

For once, he didn't seem to mind being called by his nickname. He snuggled into Faith's arms and purred. The warmth of his small body soothed her a little.

When she reached the end of the north dock, Officer Bryan Laddy was setting up police barricades. Brooke, Laura, and Wolfe waited on the other side.

The tall, slim young man was Brooke's favorite police officer, and she looked moon-eyed as she talked to him. Then she turned to Faith. "Officer Laddy wouldn't let us come after you."

"We don't want gawkers ruining the crime scene," Officer Laddy said. He was as by-the-book as an officer could get.

"My friends and I aren't gawkers," Brooke retorted. "We were worried about Faith."

Officer Laddy's cheeks, already flushed from the cold, turned a deeper red. "I didn't mean you folks. I meant, you know, strangers."

Faith rounded the barricades, still carrying the cat.

"I see you found Watson," Wolfe said.

"Thank goodness," Faith replied. "I can't imagine how he got to town or why he was on the dock."

"You're shivering." Wolfe removed his gray wool coat and draped it over Faith's shoulders. Underneath he wore a cardigan in a shade of blue that matched his eyes. This was remarkably informal attire for a man who typically wore a suit.

Faith decided the casual look worked well for Wolfe, even if he wore a dress shirt and a tie under the cardigan.

"I can take Laura back to the manor," Brooke offered.

"There's no need for you to make an extra trip." Faith began to feel warm and safe, wrapped in Wolfe's coat. "I can drop her off."

"And let us miss out on the details?" Brooke asked. "I don't think so. Laura and I will meet you at your cottage. I'll make hot chocolate."

The cat was still determined to achieve his goal of seeing a whale, even if his first attempt had ended in witnessing a murder instead.

The police officers had been unnecessarily tough with his human. She didn't have anything to do with the person's death, and in any event, she lacked the strength to throw the weapon that distance.

The cat was happy when his person tucked him inside her borrowed coat. He purred with relief. He had been concerned about hitching a ride back to the manor. Just because he'd been able to slip aboard the van once didn't guarantee he could manage the return trip. The journey was a long hike on cat legs, and the snow was still falling.

Perhaps there was a whale-viewing location closer to home. A safer place, where humans didn't spear each other with whaling implements.

Hot chocolate seemed like a standard sort of beverage, but with Brooke making it, the result was decadent and scrumptious. After a warming mug, Faith calmed down. She was grateful Brooke and Laura sat with her until her nervous shivering stopped.

Brooke set her mug on the table and leaned forward. "Now tell us exactly what happened."

After Faith explained the events of the evening and the three women finished every drop of Brooke's hot chocolate, Faith's friends left the cottage for the refuge of their own homes.

When they were gone, Faith settled in a comfy chair beside the fireplace. She opened a notebook and jotted down what had happened, including her impressions. The police officers had said they might need to question her again, and Faith wanted to get the details down before time and imagination either dimmed or embellished them.

When she finished, she retreated to her bedroom. Before she drifted off to sleep with Watson cuddled next to her, her final thoughts nearly jarred her awake again.

Had she been only feet away from someone complicit in murder?

Faith felt like she had just dozed off when her cell phone chirped on the bedside table, startling her from a dream about being on a whaling ship. Instead of hunting whales, harpoons had been raining down all around her. Thankfully, the phone woke her before any harpoons struck. She was safe in bed with Watson.

Faith glanced at the clock. Seven o'clock. It was too early, considering she had been up past midnight. Faith fumbled for her cell phone.

The call was from Marlene Russell, the assistant manager of Castleton Manor. The woman did not have much of a personal life, and she seemed to think none of her employees did either. Or she didn't care if they did. Her dedication to Castleton was admirable, but her interactions with staff could be gruff.

"Hello?" Faith knew she sounded groggy. Marlene had no doubt already been hard at work for an hour or more.

"There will be an employee meeting at eight in the music room," Marlene stated crisply.

Before a literary conference, Marlene usually touched base with a handful of staff members. But they could all fit into Marlene's basement office, so she must be planning to have the entire staff present for this meeting.

"Is there something I should know about?" Faith asked.

"You're the one who should be filling me in," Marlene said. "You're the murder witness."

My, word got around fast. "I didn't actually see anything," Faith admitted. "I don't even know who was killed."

"I'm glad you know so little. We don't need gossip and wild rumors circulating around the manor and disturbing our conference attendees."

After Marlene hung up, Faith sighed and swung her legs out of her warm cocoon of covers.

Watson yawned, exposing tiny sharp teeth and a pink tongue.

"It's rare for me to wake up before you. Last night must have worn you out." Not for the first time, Faith wished her cat could talk.

Even though Watson clearly wanted to sleep in, he stretched and jumped off the bed. Faith gladly would have slept a few more minutes herself.

Watson tucked into his breakfast as if he hadn't eaten in days. Faith didn't think she would have an appetite after what she had witnessed, but she had no trouble finishing her English muffin and poached egg.

She peeked outside to see bright sunshine. Last night's snow was already melting.

Faith dressed in a wool skirt and jacket, just in case it wasn't as warm outside as it looked. She wrapped a shawl around her shoulders that Aunt Eileen had knitted. Faith planned to call her as soon as she was settled in at work.

A love of books seemed to run in her family's blood. Eileen was head librarian at the Candle House Library in downtown Lighthouse Bay.

As she opened the front door to the cottage, Watson tried to dart past her legs.

Faith blocked the doorway. "You need to stay home. I don't want you running to town again. I won't be there to save you today."

Watson sat and gave Faith a disgruntled look. He almost seemed to be saying he had no plans to run to town, and even if he did, he would not need to be rescued.

Faith opened the door a crack and squeezed through the narrow opening, but it was no good.

Watson slipped past and dashed across the lawn, leaving a trail of prints in places where the sun had not yet melted away the snow.

Faith still had cobwebs in her brain as she entered the music room.

But Marlene seemed as fresh and sharp as always. The assistant manager scanned the room, most likely taking a head count and noting any missing employees. Not one wavy blonde hair on her head was out of place. Her trim black suit did not show a single wrinkle or speck of lint. Her ever-present expression of slight disapproval was firmly in place.

The elegantly appointed room seemed inappropriate for an employee meeting, but it was probably the only one available during a conference. Every one of the plush velvet chairs was taken.

An older gentleman with a black beard and wearing a worn canvas work coat stood so Faith could take his seat. She thanked him. He worked at the Jaxons' private boat dock, but she didn't know his name.

Marlene rapped a pen against her coffee mug, drawing attention to where she stood.

The quiet chattering stopped.

"As many of you have already heard, one of our guests passed away last night," Marlene announced without preamble.

Faith felt a ripple of dread crawl up her spine.

"As employees of the manor, you may be asked for details about this unfortunate incident." Marlene focused on Faith. "I should not have to tell you that we do not need ugly rumors sullying our sterling reputation. Any inquiries should be directed to me. Are there any questions?"

The head of housekeeping raised her hand. "Who is the deceased?" she asked.

Faith bit her lower lip, afraid of the answer.

Marlene's expression conveyed that she had not expected anyone to ask such a tasteless question. She emitted a disappointed sigh. "I suppose the staff needs to know, if only so you won't be startled by guests asking after the recently departed. We must appear to be on top of things at all times." She cleared her throat. "The deceased is Raymond Prather."

4

Faith gasped, then clapped a hand over her mouth.

Marlene didn't provide any details about Raymond's death, but Faith knew he had been murdered last night on the north dock in Lighthouse Bay.

The assistant manager delivered a few more instructions that bordered on threats, commanding the staff to refrain from spreading rumors about Raymond's untimely demise.

That order would be easy to follow. Faith had been there, and she knew next to nothing. No one else present could have more information than she did. Unless the harpoon thrower and the man in the walrus mustache were manor employees.

Marlene dismissed the meeting, and Faith exited the music room with the rest of the staff. As she headed into the gallery, she heard raised voices.

Lou Bennett stood with his hands on his hips. Today he resembled a museum director, not a ship's captain in the 1800s. He wore a tweed jacket, and his fake walrus mustache was gone. "I rushed right over when I heard it was missing."

One of the vendors pointed to an empty space in a tall display case. "It was right there when I left last night."

Marlene pushed her way through the cluster of vendors to the two men. "What's missing?"

"The harpoon," Lou said. "We loaned it for display during your conference in the belief it was perfectly secure. Now it's gone."

Faith didn't hear Marlene's attempt at damage control. She hurried the rest of the way through the gallery and unlocked the library with shaking hands. She closed and locked the door behind her. The library wasn't scheduled to open for another thirty minutes. Faith needed every one of those minutes to calm herself.

She sank into her chair, placed her elbows on her desk, and lowered her face into her hands. She shuddered, trying not to relive those terrible moments on the dock just hours before.

A long, slender object with a rope trailing it had sliced through the falling snow, plunging into Raymond Prather. A bloody drag mark marred the dock, the result of the murderer removing the weapon.

Raymond had been murdered with the whaling museum's harpoon. A thief had stolen the antique weapon from the manor.

Faith jumped up, pushing her chair back with an inelegant squeak. She rushed to the locked display cases containing Jaxon family treasures and the irreplaceable Hawaiian artifacts Tasi had set out. Faith studied both cases, searching for any empty spaces that would mean the harpoon thief had somehow managed to plunder them too.

She was relieved to find that they were undisturbed.

A soft rapping on the library door drew Faith's attention away from her visual inventory. She opened the door a crack, not quite ready to share her space with conference attendees.

Laura peeked in, her face creased with worry.

Faith opened the door to allow Laura inside, then quickly closed and locked it again.

Laura wore her housekeeping uniform—black pants and a white shirt. "Have you seen Mr. Prather's briefcase?" she asked.

"His briefcase?" Then Faith remembered. Yesterday he had clutched it possessively, refusing to divulge its contents to Tasi or Milton. "I haven't noticed it around. Why do you ask?"

"After the meeting, I went to the second floor to tidy the hallway before guests went to breakfast," Laura answered. "Mrs. Prather burst out of her room. She just noticed the briefcase is missing from their room, and she's frantic. She said something about a scrimshaw."

"The *Essex* scrimshaw," Faith said. "It's very valuable. I doubt we'll find it here because I kept the library locked, but we can look."

Laura climbed the spiral steps to investigate the second level of the library, and Faith searched the ground floor. They examined every cubbyhole, drawer, and shelf that would hold a briefcase but with no luck. Faith imagined all the secret passages in the manor and considered how easy it would be to hide Raymond's briefcase.

"If a thief only wanted the scrimshaw," Faith told Laura, "they may have discarded the briefcase."

"Should we search the trash cans behind the kitchen?" Laura asked.

"We've both spent enough time away from our jobs this morning. I need to open the library, and I don't want you getting scolded by Marlene. We should tell the police, though."

"In case Mr. Prather's death and the stolen scrimshaw are related?"

Faith had no idea why Raymond would be sneaking around the north dock at night or whether he'd had the briefcase at the time, but it made sense that the man in the shadows with him or the person pitching the harpoon might have stolen the scrimshaw. Which meant either could have seen Faith on the dock. She hadn't been able to identify Raymond's companion or the harpoon thrower, but the killer might not realize that.

If the missing harpoon was the murder weapon, then the thief had access to the manor. As a guest, an employee, or a vendor?

Suddenly the library didn't feel like a safe haven anymore.

Fortunately, the conference had begun by the time Chief Garris arrived. While guests were busy attending talks about whaling, New England literature of the early 1800s, and the novel *Moby-Dick* in other areas of the manor, the police attempted discretion by interviewing employees in the somewhat remote den. That only served to disrupt Faith's day as a steady stream of people walked through the library to enter or exit the room.

When it was her turn, Faith made sure Laura was available to watch the library in her absence. Knowing there might be a thief at Castleton Manor had made Faith paranoid. She was responsible for the Jaxon family's precious collection of first editions.

Faith repeated the information she had given to Officer Rooney and Chief Garris the previous night, but she added her newly hatched theories.

"You know the harpoon on loan from the whaling museum is missing," Faith said. "Someone with access to the manor must have stolen it from the gallery last night."

"I'm asking the questions," Chief Garris reminded her.

"If the harpoon is the murder weapon . . ." Faith paused for a beat to see whether Chief Garris would confirm her suspicion, but his expression might as well have been carved in granite for all it revealed to her. It was probably something he learned in the Marines. She gave up and finished the thought herself. "Then whoever stole the harpoon has access to the manor."

"Thanks for your insight," Garris said, "but that's a very long list of suspects. Rest assured, we're investigating every possibility."

The chief's words were probably intended to warn Faith away from meddling with their investigation, something she'd been accused of more than once, but she continued anyway.

"Did you hear that Mrs. Prather's potentially valuable scrimshaw is missing?" Faith asked. "Maybe stolen?"

Something flickered across Chief Garris's face. Whether it was interest or annoyance, Faith wasn't sure.

"Did you witness a discussion between Raymond Prather, Tasi Kekoa, and Milton Waldrin yesterday?" he asked.

"Here in the library?" Faith asked.

Chief Garris remained silent.

"Yes, I did," Faith said. "But getting back to the harpoon—"

"I'm more interested in the conversation between the three conference guests," the chief interrupted. "Can you tell me what they talked about?"

Faith recalled harsh words. Raymond had insulted both Tasi and Milton. Tasi had obviously taken offense, and Milton had played peacekeeper. As carefully and honestly as she could, she told Chief Garris what she remembered.

Perhaps Tasi or Milton was considered a murder suspect.

The cat strolled through the first floor of the manor. As multiple talks ended, conference attendees flooded the Great Hall Gallery. The owners of Castleton Manor wisely encouraged their guests to bring pets, and the cat took this opportunity to observe the newcomers. Felines, canines, a parakeet, and a ferret mingled with their humans, making small talk in the form of polite sniffing.

Across the crowded room, he noticed a feline of the feminine persuasion. An exotic human cradled a Persian cat with gloriously long, white fur, vivid blue eyes, and the loveliest pink nose he had ever seen. She glanced around the room, taking in the activity from her secure perch.

He struck a pose, willing her to meet his gaze.

Instead, her attention was diverted by a salmon puff hors d'oeuvre offered to her by her person from a small plate of gourmet treats intended for human consumption. A sizable chunk of the pastry tumbled to the floor.

The cat swiftly zigzagged through a hazardous maze of shifting human legs and feet to reach the Persian. He hoped to make her acquaintance. Failing that, he aimed to capture the piece of salmon puff.

But before he reached his goal, he ran into an immovable obstacle. Or rather, it ran into him. The unusually short canine nearly knocked the cat over in his haste to scarf up the salmon puff. Typical dog—he inhaled the delicate pastry so quickly that he couldn't have tasted it.

The cat's disgust and disappointment must have vibrated from his whiskers, because the dog turned, flinching away from his gaze.

How a fellow so powerfully built could be so timid was beyond the cat's comprehension. He attempted to put the dog at ease by sitting and licking one paw, indicating that he had not been much disturbed by his appalling lack of manners.

In response, the dog swiped a wet, salmon-flavored tongue across the cat's impeccably groomed face.

The police concluded their interviews in the den, packed up, and left the manor. Faith kept busy as guests wandered into the library to admire the book collection in its beautiful surroundings. When the next conference sessions began, the library emptied.

Chief Garris did not seem interested in Faith's insights, but she could accomplish something the police could not—observe their two suspects in the relaxed atmosphere of the conference, where the killer might let his or her guard down.

Faith found Laura on break between duties and asked her to watch the library for a little while. Laura was happy to sit in for her as she did her college homework. While Marlene didn't exactly approve of Faith borrowing Laura from housekeeping, she had given up trying to end the arrangement. Especially when Wolfe supported Laura's finishing her degree in library science.

Faith consulted the conference program. Milton was scheduled to give his lecture "The Truth Behind the *Essex* Tragedy" that afternoon. Tasi was currently speaking about the prehistory of the Polynesian peoples in the salon.

Faith had seen how upset Raymond had made Tasi when he implied she was not qualified to inspect the *Essex* scrimshaw. Had she been angry enough to kill?

Faith approached the salon quietly and peeked into the room, trying not to disturb Tasi's talk.

Tasi stood behind a podium and delivered her speech with lively enthusiasm, relating Polynesian myths in an engaging storytelling style. Her hair was arranged with ivory combs, and she wore a colorful dress that flattered her figure. Despite Tasi's striking looks and obvious femininity, Faith imagined the tall woman could probably throw a harpoon as easily as any man.

A table beside Tasi held a collection of artifacts similar to those on display in the library, with the addition of a huge wooden mask bearing a frightening grimace. Faith glimpsed what appeared to be a feathery white boa draped beneath the table. She crouched a bit and realized it was a fluffy Persian cat seated on a chair.

Faith glanced around and was startled to see Watson behind a potted fern, his gaze riveted on the Persian. But she was relieved he was safe inside the manor and not gallivanting off to the docks.

As Tasi spoke, Faith scanned the audience. Even more surprising than seeing Watson was noticing Judith and Agnes in the crowd. Faith had expected the sisters to leave the conference right away. She decided they must be made of sterner stuff than the average woman to be sitting in a lecture just hours after Raymond's death.

Or maybe Judith hoped her *Essex* scrimshaw would turn up.

The lecture was nearing its end, judging by the time and Tasi's request for audience questions.

Judith rose and worked her way to the aisle between chairs. Her hair, while tidy in a silver bob, seemed to droop around her thin face.

Agnes got up, gripping her ivory-handled cane. Her black slacks emphasized her rail-thin legs under the pretty rose tunic that hung from her wide shoulders. Agnes followed her sister out of the room.

Faith met them right outside the door. "Words aren't adequate, but I am so sorry for your loss," she told them. "If there is anything we can do for you, please let us know."

Agnes's eyes met Faith's, her expression hard as flint. "Have they made any progress?"

Faith wasn't sure what Agnes meant or how much the police had told them about Raymond's murder. Faith had been warned by both the police and Marlene not to share information with guests.

"The scrimshaw," Agnes said impatiently. "Do the police have any leads?"

Faith was not a psychologist, but she thought it was safe to attribute Agnes's odd response to shock. The woman could not process her brother-in-law's recent death and instead focused on the loss of the scrimshaw. Or perhaps Agnes showed little emotion in any circumstance.

"Not that I know of. But they are working diligently to find out what happened," she answered, keeping her response vague.

"I was told Castleton Manor was a perfectly safe place to visit." Agnes narrowed her eyes in an expression of anger, not sorrow. "As well as Lighthouse Bay. 'No safer town on the East Coast,' people said. And then this happens on our first night here. A common thief prowling the halls, victimizing innocent citizens."

Judith had been silent during the entire exchange. Now she rested her hand on Agnes's arm and said, "Calm down."

Agnes jerked away. "I will not. That scrimshaw is an important artifact for our family. And I warned you not to marry that man," she spat, then turned and stormed away, her cane thumping on the floor.

Surprised at the outburst, Faith stared after Agnes.

Judith turned to Faith. "Please excuse my sister. She never married, and she's always been jealous of Raymond and me."

Faith wasn't sure how to respond to Judith's admission, so she glanced around the room. She realized that Tasi's lecture had ended as people rose from their seats and collected their belongings. Faith had only a few more undisturbed moments with Judith.

"How can you be so certain it was stolen from the manor?" Faith asked. "Are you sure Raymond didn't have the scrimshaw with him on the dock?"

Judith cocked her head, as though Faith's suggestion had not occurred to her. "I suppose that is a possibility."

"Why was Raymond on the dock?" Faith asked.

Judith staggered backward, as though the weight of her grief might topple her to the floor.

Faith's heart went out to the woman, and she rested a hand on her arm to steady her.

But Judith pulled away from her touch. "He was lured to his doom by a scrimshander."

5

Faith wondered if the scrimshander, or scrimshaw artist, who had lured Raymond to the dock might be staying at the manor. Charlotte had insisted on extending a welcome to anyone interested in seeing the educational exhibit from the whaling museum.

The vendors were delighted to offer their whaling-related wares to a larger clientele than just the conference attendees. Faith made her way through the packed Great Hall Gallery, unable to tell who among the crowd were locals and who were from out of town. Some conference attendees had rooms in nearby bed-and-breakfasts or at hotels in Lighthouse Bay. Those guests lucky enough to stay in the manor were ensconced in the eighteen suites on the second floor.

Maybe Agnes had a valid point. With so many visitors, the limited security personnel would have a difficult time keeping an eye on everyone. A thief could easily mingle with the crowd, then slip away to hide somewhere in the huge mansion, sneaking out later to steal the harpoon and break into the Prathers' suite.

The antique harpoon had been stolen from the gallery the previous night. Judith had not ruled out that Raymond might have had the *Essex* scrimshaw with him on the north dock, but she hadn't noticed it was missing until this morning. That was understandable, considering her husband had been murdered less than twenty-four hours ago.

So, had the *Essex* scrimshaw been stolen by the man with the walrus mustache on the dock, or was it taken from Judith's room in the manor?

Faith did not have time to dwell on the mystery. She was too busy fielding questions about the library, the manor, and the murder. Curious visitors seemed to think Faith would willingly spill everything she knew about Raymond's demise, as if librarians were required to divulge facts on demand.

Faith concentrated on her role as librarian. Friday passed quickly, and soon she was locking the library doors.

Just as she dropped the key into her jacket pocket, Watson trotted up to her.

"Are you as ready to go home as I am?" Faith picked up the cat, who tucked his head under her chin and purred. "I'm glad you didn't make me search for you. I don't have any energy left after the busy day I had."

Exhausted from the previous night's events, she walked straight to her cottage. After a quick dinner and a tunaroon for Watson, cat and human turned in early.

The next day, Faith was grateful for the refreshing night's sleep. Every visitor to Castleton Manor seemed to find their way to the library Saturday morning.

Faith wished she could call on Laura to help, but she didn't dare upset Marlene by keeping Laura from her housekeeping duties any more than she already had. The college student needed her job, and Faith was determined to remain on Marlene's good side. If she had ever truly been there.

Faith struggled to remain patient and helpful and to maintain her typical cheerful attitude. Some of the questions people asked reminded her of drivers slowing on a highway to gawk at a horrific traffic accident.

After she finished telling yet another guest that she had no information to share concerning Raymond's death, she turned and jumped. She hadn't seen Milton and his dachshund, Boomer, approach her desk. Both wore their signature bow ties at a slightly skewed angle. Their matching herringbone tweed jackets were adorable.

Faith recovered quickly. "Mr. Waldrin, how may I help you?"

"I wondered if it would be possible to see the SS *Honoria*'s log up close. I would like to verify the weather on a particular date."

"That's a very interesting request." Faith was relieved he required assistance with a task actually suited to her duties as a librarian.

"I'm contributing to an article for a historical journal," Milton explained. "The author claims a merchant ship sank in a storm on a certain date, and I promised to check original source material to verify there was a storm on that date. I've read elsewhere that Captain Jaxon was usually in that area around that time of year, and you can't get more original than a ship captain's log."

"I'm happy to help a fellow researcher." Faith opened a desk drawer and retrieved the display case key. As she did, she realized that she had just revealed the location of the key to a possible thief and murder suspect. She would now have to carry the keys with her until the conference was over.

Faith handed Milton a pair of white cloth gloves. "You'll need to wear these to handle the log."

"Of course." Milton tugged on the gloves.

Faith put on a pair of similar gloves. She turned the key in the cabinet lock, raised the hinged glass top of the display case, then lifted the log from its easel.

As Faith set the leather-bound book on a nearby table, Milton whispered, "Oh my."

"Is that a whaling ship log?" a nearby visitor asked.

"The SS *Honoria* was a merchant ship," Faith said, "not a whaler. It carried goods along the New England coast as well as across the Atlantic Ocean. It went to and from England and France. Whaling ships followed the whales and often spent time in tropical regions."

Milton smiled. "Not many people are so knowledgeable in my area of expertise." Then he returned his attention to the log.

Boomer settled at Milton's feet, placing his black snout on top of his stubby legs.

"Can I see a whaling ship log?" the visitor asked.

"Unfortunately, there aren't any original whaling ship logs in this collection." Faith waved a hand at the two stories of bookcases. "We do have many reprints available, though. You're welcome to read one of them while you're visiting the library."

"That's okay." The guest pointed at a bookshelf. "I saw this one at a booth in the gallery. I'll buy my own copy from him."

The crowd thinned as they neared lunchtime. Faith's stomach growled, but she couldn't leave the library while a valuable item from the archives was in the possession of a guest.

It was just as well Faith was still on duty, because Tasi entered the library, cradling her Persian cat in her arms like a human infant.

The fluffy cat appeared totally at ease, casting a languid but intelligent look around the room. The cat probably thought she deserved the luxurious surroundings.

"What a lovely Persian," Faith said.

"This is my Alika," Tasi said proudly. "It means 'most beautiful.' Fortunately, it's relatively easy to bring companion animals from Hawaii to the mainland and back again. I can't go anywhere without her."

"I can understand not wanting to leave her behind when you travel," Faith said. "So how may I help you?"

"If it's not too much trouble, I would like to retrieve an item from my display case," Tasi answered. "I need it for my talk this afternoon."

Faith complied, happy to assist the lovely Polynesian woman, even if she was a murder suspect. Faith was alone in the library with two possible killers, but she had a difficult time imagining either one killing Raymond with a harpoon. Still, she was glad there was activity in the gallery outside the open library doors. Faith had to be safe with all the visitors and vendors within hearing distance. She hoped.

Watson trailed Tasi, his gaze fixed on the white Persian in the woman's arms. When Tasi set Alika carefully on a velvet sofa, Watson approached, strutting in his best debonair style.

Faith was amused to realize her cat was attempting to impress the Persian. When Boomer nosed in, Faith guessed from the way Watson's stump of a tail twitched that the dachshund was an unwelcome intruder.

After Tasi removed an ancient, delicate basket from the display, Faith began to lower the glass top.

"Wait just a minute."

Faith nearly jumped a foot at the abrupt voice, followed by the thumping of a cane on the carpet.

"I need to examine those cases," Agnes stated.

Faith closed the glass display case cover and turned the key in the lock. She stepped aside. "The displays are available for all guests to view."

"I'm looking for my sister's *Essex* scrimshaw," Agnes said.

"It's not in my case," Tasi snapped.

"And it's not amongst the Jaxon family antiquities," Faith added.

"I'll be the judge of that," Agnes said. "Open those cases. I need to make sure it's not hidden under some of this other junk."

Tasi threw herself in front of her display, blocking Agnes. "Why would your scrimshaw be in with my artifacts?"

"You can answer that better than I can," Agnes said. "Step aside and let me see."

"First of all, I can't allow you to paw through the delicate treasures from my people's past," Tasi said, her voice rising in anger.

Faith noticed that Tasi used the word *paw*, the same term that Raymond had used when he'd insulted both Tasi and Milton.

"And second," Tasi went on, "I deeply resent your implication."

"Please, ladies." Milton rose from his seat at the table. "May I offer my services as a disinterested third party?"

Agnes snorted in derision. "You want the *Essex* scrimshaw as badly as anyone," she accused. "Why should I trust you to search for it?"

"If someone took your sister's scrimshaw," Faith said, "I would not expect him or her to put it on display." Besides, she and Laura had already done a thorough search of the library, but Faith wasn't about to admit that to the irate woman.

"What better place to hide a stolen valuable than in plain sight?" As Agnes took a sudden step closer to the display case, she nearly stumbled over Boomer.

The dachshund yelped.

The cat almost couldn't believe his eyes. He was, however, a keen observer of life, and he was certain he was not mistaken. The human swung at the dog with her cane. The poor fellow cried out in terror, then bolted toward the library door.

The cat chased after him. Running away was not the right method to deal with difficult situations.

The dog darted between and around the sea of human legs crowding the gallery. Before the canine escaped out the front entrance of the manor, the human who made many tasty treats stopped him. Uttering soothing words, she carefully picked up the long fellow and carried him back to the library.

The cat was distressed that his new friend, however annoying he might be, could have been harmed.

Justice was in order.

Milton rushed up to Brooke and took Boomer from her. He held the dachshund in his arms. The bow ties on both owner and pup were even more skewed than before.

"I can't thank you enough," Milton told her. "If Boomer tried to run down those front steps, he could have hurt his back. Dachshunds are at particular risk for spinal injuries."

"It was no trouble at all," Brooke said, "although now I'll have to change my jacket." An oily spot and dark dog hair marred her snow-white chef's coat. She turned to Faith. "I was bringing you a turkey wrap left over from lunch, but it got squished when I picked up this sweet puppy. And he might have taken a bite. Or two."

Boomer swiped his pink tongue around his muzzle and wagged his tail.

"Are you okay, Boom-Boom?" Milton studied the dog, then shook his head. "I don't understand why Boomer would run off like that."

Faith thought she knew. Milton had not been able to see the entire drama from the table, but she was pretty sure Agnes had swung her cane at Boomer. The woman made no apologies, so perhaps it had been an accident.

"All this fuss over a dog," Agnes scoffed. "He seems sturdy enough."

Milton looked wounded, in the way only a pet owner who truly loves his animal companion can when his furry friend is dismissed as having no importance.

"I can see I'll get no cooperation from any of you," Agnes continued. "I'm going to speak to the assistant manager." She thumped her cane once on the carpet.

Terrific. All Faith needed was to be on Marlene's bad side. Or was it her *worse* side?

Watson trotted over to Agnes, weaving his way around her ankles.

Faith wondered why her cat had taken a sudden liking to Agnes.

When Agnes jerked one foot away from Watson, he simply turned his kitty massage technique to her other ankle.

Faith reached for Watson, but before she could get her hands on him, Agnes attempted to step over him. The tangle of legs and cat ended with Agnes falling against the display case. When Tasi held her arm to keep her from tumbling to the floor, Agnes jerked away from the younger woman.

"Don't touch me!" She jabbed a shaking finger in Watson's direction. "I'll make certain that creature doesn't trip anyone else!"

Faith's apologies fell on deaf ears as Agnes barreled out of the library. No doubt the woman was headed straight to Marlene's office.

Faith felt anger boiling up. Why did people who hated pets stay at a literary retreat that advertised itself as a pet-friendly establishment? She took a deep breath and calmed herself. Agnes had just lost her brother-in-law. Some people reacted to sorrow by acting out in anger. Faith needed to make allowances for the woman.

She picked up Watson, holding him tight in her arms. "What were you thinking?"

6

As expected, Faith received a call from Marlene, ordering her to meet in her office as soon as possible. Faith delayed the meeting as she waited for Milton to finish his research. All too soon, he returned the ship log to Faith and left.

She locked the library. If she hurried, she could drop by the kitchen on her way to see if Brooke might have another leftover wrap to spare. Faith was fiercely hungry, but she had no time to run home for lunch.

As she passed through the gallery, another thought quieted her growling stomach. The empty spot in the museum display left by the missing harpoon had been filled with a replica harpoon. The real harpoon had been stolen Thursday night. The conference started Friday morning, and most of the attendees had checked in then.

While Lighthouse Bay citizens and tourists had been encouraged to view the whaling display at the manor, only registered guests were allowed in after normal business hours. The killer had to be among the guests who had arrived early. Unless the murderer was a Castleton Manor employee, a vendor, or even a local resident who hid in the gallery before the manor doors were closed for the evening.

Faith paused beside the statue of Dame Agatha Christie in the Great Hall Gallery. Means, motive, and opportunity were the keys to solving a mystery. Faith had convinced herself dozens of people had the means—access to steal the murder weapon—but few would have the motive to kill Raymond. And even fewer people had the opportunity to throw the harpoon across the north dock.

Making a detour to the lobby, Faith strolled to the conference registration desk. The long table, covered with a maroon cloth, was manned by volunteers. With the initial rush of registration over and the conference lectures in full swing, the volunteers had wandered away. Someone probably scooted out to assist attendees between sessions.

Faith had only a few minutes until the next classes ended. Where to start? A plastic filing box held folders with each conference attendee's name printed neatly on the tab. Attendees might be staying at Castleton Manor, a nearby bed-and-breakfast, or a Lighthouse Bay hotel. It would take too long to go through the 150 or so files.

Faith noticed a printout of several pages that was stapled in the upper left corner. The names of guests who had received their conference packets were highlighted. Faith turned the printout around and thumbed through the pages. Fortunately, the list was color coded: green highlight for attendees checking in Thursday, blue for Friday, and pink for today.

Milton Waldrin, Raymond and Judith Prather, Agnes VanStuth, and Tasi Kekoa were highlighted in green, but Faith already knew they had arrived early. Three other people had picked up their packets Thursday, but from the notations by their names, they were all staying elsewhere.

Faith wished she had better detecting skills. The information told her nothing. Maybe knowing where the guests were Thursday night would be more revealing. Had they been in their rooms? Or wandering around the docks in Lighthouse Bay? Laura might be able to tell her who had stayed at the manor and who had gone out for the evening, but Faith would have to be careful not to get the young woman in trouble.

Conference attendees began shuffling out of the meeting rooms in groups of twos and threes, headed for the refreshment tables in the Great Hall.

Faith turned the list around quickly and headed for Marlene's office on the basement level.

The cat could tell his human was troubled. As she went downstairs, he trotted up the curving staircase to the second floor. He sniffed along the corridor until he located the room containing his new canine friend.

The cat sat on the plush carpeting, casually grooming his paw, until a human pushed a cart in front of the door. She knocked, announced her presence, then used a key to enter the room. The cat followed. The person never noticed as she fussed around the room.

The dog was inside a wire cage, cushioned with a padded bed and plenty of blankets and toys, but it was a cage nonetheless. He sat up and pressed his snout between the bars.

The cat approached the dog, and they briefly touched noses in greeting before the cat batted the door latch with his paw. He was skilled in the ways of escaping confinement. While the human ran a vacuum—a hideously noisy device both he and his friend cringed from—the cat handily dealt with the latch. The door swung open. The cat took two paces toward the open room door, then turned.

The dog huddled inside the cage. He probably feared running into the woman with the stick.

The human returned to the sitting room. The cat had just enough time to hide under a chair. She spoke to the dog, surprise in her voice, then closed his cage. The Mystery of the Unlatched Cage would be one the person would never solve.

The person spoke softly, rattling on in the inefficient wordiness of humans, but the sounds appeared to soothe the dog. Then the human placed room service trays containing traces of last night's dinner and this morning's breakfast dishes, judging from the smells, onto her cart, even though the manor offered delectable meals downstairs.

The cat suspected that the dog's person hid in his room in the same way the dog hid in his cage.

Faith closed the door to Marlene's office behind her. She would have liked to give it a quick tug to make it slam shut, but Faith knew better than to antagonize the assistant manager.

Watson was not allowed in the manor until Agnes left the conference. Although Marlene seemed to relish delivering the ultimatum, Faith knew she was just placating Agnes. Maybe if Faith found the scrimshaw or the murderer or both, Judith and Agnes would leave, and Watson could regain his right to wander the manor at will.

She walked to the library, wondering how she could comply with Marlene's demand to temporarily banish Watson from the premises. Her cat was full of surprises and tended to appear wherever he wanted. Even so, she was determined to do her best to keep him at home.

As she passed the vendor tables, Faith noticed a woman examining the pretty ivory hair comb she had admired Thursday. The woman held it next to her honey-blonde hair, glanced in a handheld mirror, then shook her head.

"It's too light," the woman said, disappointment in her voice. "The comb is beautiful, but it disappears against my hair."

Faith paused a moment too long, watching the vendor place the comb back in the display.

The friendly woman saw her, then motioned for Faith to come closer. "That was the third woman to try it on. None had quite the right hair color to show off such a lovely ivory comb. Yours provides the perfect contrast." She pulled the comb from the case and held it out to Faith.

Faith began to reach for the comb, then pulled her hand back. "I can't. Really. It's beautiful, but—"

"Maybe if other women see how it looks in your hair," the vendor said, "they'll realize what a treasure it is."

That's the problem. Faith felt a pang of regret that she might help sell the comb when she found it so appealing.

"I would like to see it," a man's voice said.

Wolfe was a commanding presence wherever he went, not a man easily overlooked. Faith must have been completely mesmerized by the comb, because Wolfe had appeared at her side unnoticed.

"My mother's hair is dark," Wolfe continued. "The comb would be a nice gift."

Faith accepted the comb from the vendor's soft hands, then twisted it into her long hair.

The vendor handed her a mirror. "Beautiful," the woman said. "It was made for auburn hair."

"You said it was made in 1853," Faith murmured. "Imagine something this delicate lasting all that time." She removed it from her hair and handed it back to the vendor. Maybe if Wolfe purchased it for his mother, she wouldn't feel as disappointed about not having it for herself. "Thank you for letting me try it on."

Wolfe followed Faith to the library. She unlocked the door, and they walked inside.

Faith stepped behind her desk. "May I help you with something today?"

"I need to retrieve a piece from the display," Wolfe replied. "Mr. Waldrin and Ms. Kekoa are both scrimshaw experts. I want to know whether one of mine is whalebone or ivory. I've always assumed ivory, but why not let a knowledgeable person confirm that for me? I mean, especially since they're both here anyway."

Faith pulled her keys out of her pocket and unlocked the case. "Does it matter which material is used?"

"Ivory is more valuable. And rare. After endangered species laws and import regulations were passed to protect whales and elephants from extinction, ivory became difficult to acquire. I verify the provenance of scrimshaw in my collection, of course. I wouldn't want to purchase illegal or poached materials."

"Absolutely not," Faith said. "I'm glad the whaling museum is going to support whale protection."

Wolfe studied the open display case for a moment, then pulled out a piece decorated with the delicate carving of a ship with three masts, the canvas sails curved as though filled with a strong wind. "This is a confirmed historical piece," he said. "Perhaps now I'll know for certain which material the artist used."

After Wolfe left, Faith searched the library for Watson. She expected to find him sleeping in one of his favorite spots, but the cat was nowhere to be found. She hoped he wasn't getting into more trouble. Working in the library wouldn't be as enjoyable if she couldn't spend her days with Watson at her side.

The rest of the day fell into a rhythm of influxes of guests between conference talks, followed by lulls during which Faith straightened up the seating areas and shelved books.

After the last session of the day and before dinner, Wolfe returned the scrimshaw to his display case.

"What was the verdict?" Faith asked. "Whalebone or ivory?"

"Ivory, as I thought. The scrimshaw was among the items in Angus Jaxon's estate. It may have been carved by a sailor employed on Angus's merchant ship."

"That is a treasure, then," Faith said. "Not just as valuable scrimshaw but as family history too." She closed the case and locked it. "Do you think the *Essex* scrimshaw was real?"

"We may never know," Wolfe said. "Unless it's found and examined by an expert."

"Poor Mrs. Prather. She said she spent her savings on it. It must have cost a fortune."

"I hope for her sake she had it insured. Although without being authenticated, the insurance company might balk at paying out more than the cost of scrimshaw like mine." Wolfe waved a hand at the locked case.

He obviously knew a lot about the value of scrimshaw and the importance of insuring his collection. That made Faith feel a little more relaxed about her responsibility, but she would still exercise every caution to keep the library locked when she was not present. She knew the actual pieces of his family history were more important to Wolfe than any amount of money.

Watson sauntered into the library after Wolfe left.

Faith scooped the cat up into a hug. "Where have you been? Wherever you were, I hope you were behaving."

Watson purred, then struggled to be let down. Faith set him on the carpet.

Laura stepped into the library. "I'm done with housekeeping for the day. Do you need any help before I go to dinner?"

"Thanks for the offer," Faith said, "but I had enough quiet time today to stay on top of tidying up. Tomorrow afternoon might be busy again. Drop by if you can. I'm sure I'll need help."

Laura nodded and turned to go. Watson darted toward her, twining himself around her ankles. She stopped and reached down to scratch his ears. Faith was glad to see someone who didn't mind her cat.

Then she remembered the question she had meant to ask Laura. "Would you know whether a guest had been in his or her room Thursday night?"

"I was at the ship dedication party with you and Brooke."

"Yes, but the next day when you cleaned rooms—" Faith stopped and brushed a hand through her hair. Laura was a working college student, not Hercule Poirot. "Oh, never mind."

Watson planted himself firmly on the carpet and mewed.

Laura glanced at the cat. Then she smiled. "Actually, I did notice Mr. Waldrin orders room service for most of his meals. Definitely Thursday night, because I picked up the tray Friday when I cleaned his room. I thought it was odd, considering he could have eaten with the rest of the guests in the banquet hall. I would if I was a guest here. The room is amazing."

"Thanks," Faith said. "It's probably better if you don't tell Marlene I was asking about the guests."

"No problem," she said before she left.

The sun was already setting. Faith buttoned up her coat and scurried past the dormant gardens to her cottage.

Watson bounded ahead, greeting her on the threshold.

While she prepared their meals, she reviewed what she knew.

Milton had eaten Thursday night dinner in his room, but that didn't mean he hadn't stolen the harpoon later, then killed Raymond on the dock. He seemed like a nice man, but didn't people say that about their neighbors who went on murderous rampages? "He seemed like such a nice guy."

Faith felt the same way about Tasi. Although the woman had shown a temperamental streak, she had been pushed pretty far before expressing herself. Had she been pushed far enough by Raymond's insults to kill?

Who was the mysterious man on the dock with Raymond—the scrimshander, according to Judith? Was he complicit in the murder?

Faith didn't know how to pursue explanations for the boot prints, the scattered fifty-dollar bills, or the drag mark on the dock, but she could ask Corrie Baker about the receipt from her antique shop, The Fishwife's Attic.

Human and cat enjoyed dinner together. After missing lunch, Faith was ravenous. She washed up the dishes, then relaxed in front of the fireplace with a mystery novel. The cottage was warm and snug. She had begun to doze off when she heard a noise outside.

The sound of footsteps caused Watson to prick up his ears.

Faith's friends and her aunt normally called before visiting. Who would just pop by unannounced? She waited, listening, but there was no knock on the door.

Faith crept to the window, debating whether to peek out. Guests were known to wander the grounds at night. By the time she worked up the courage to yank the curtain aside, whoever had been outside the cottage was gone.

"Just a lost guest," Faith told Watson.

That night, she hugged Watson close while she slept, dreading the morning and complying with Marlene's demand that the cat be banished from the manor until Agnes left.

7

Faith dressed for church in a skirt and a soft sweater. The library would not open until eleven, giving her plenty of time to join Aunt Eileen for services and maybe even a light brunch afterward.

"Rumpy, I won't be coming back for you after church. Agnes was upset when she tripped over you. Marlene says you can't come to work with me today." Faith fought feelings of frustration and anger. "Or any day until that horrid woman—" She stopped herself. Agnes was grieving for a loved one. Faith owed her a little grace. "Until Agnes leaves the manor."

Maybe Faith gave him too much credit, but she was certain her cat understood human language, especially in tough situations. He didn't even try to rush past Faith as she squeezed out the door.

Determined to have a good attitude in spite of Watson's banishment, Faith focused on the lovely blue sky. The morning air was crisp, but the weather forecast promised mild temperatures.

Her positive attitude might have continued if she hadn't glanced to the right of the door at the flower bed. Someone had trampled through the mulch protecting last season's sleeping flower bulbs. Pressed into the frost-crusted garden soil was one perfect shoe print. Or was it a boot?

The person she had heard outside her cottage window last night hadn't been a lost guest. A normal person would have knocked and asked directions back to the manor. This one had stood facing her curtained window, possibly trying to peer inside.

Faith shivered. If she had opened the curtain or the front door, whom would she have seen? Why had someone been sneaking around outside her cottage?

Faith pulled out her phone and snapped a quick photo before the sun hit the front of the house and melted away the evidence.

Then she called the police. Officer Rooney and Chief Garris were not on duty, but Officer Mick Tobin was available. When Faith explained the situation, he agreed to come over immediately. Faith sincerely hoped she wasn't making something out of nothing.

She stepped back inside the cottage to wait, calling Eileen to explain her delay.

"You should have called the police last night," her aunt admonished. "You don't know what that person was up to. They could have broken into the cottage."

Faith regretted causing her aunt distress. Maybe she shouldn't have told Eileen about the intruder. But Lighthouse Bay was a small town, and Eileen was certain to hear about the police visiting her niece's home. Faith would have been in more trouble if she'd allowed that to happen.

"I'm sure it was nothing to worry about," Faith said. "Officer Tobin just pulled up. I don't think I'll make it to church this morning."

"I'm calling as soon as the service is over," Eileen promised.

"Better yet, I'll have a long break this afternoon. Maybe we can meet at Snickerdoodles for a late lunch."

"That sounds good. Just let me know for sure."

Faith agreed and ended the call.

Mick Tobin was an easygoing guy with a good sense of humor. The officer was in his early thirties and a bit thick around the middle. He had a relaxed manner and tended to put people at ease.

He greeted Faith, then examined the lone boot print in the flower bed. The morning sun had already softened the frost. "Not much left," he said.

"I took a picture." Faith brought up the image of the print on her phone and showed it to him.

Tobin squinted at the small screen. "It looks kind of like the print a fisherman's rubber boot would make." He squatted to inspect the remains of the print pressed into the garden mulch, then stood and studied the window.

"Great," Faith said. "That should narrow it down. A fisherman."

"Not really," the officer said. "Just about every man and a lot of women in Lighthouse Bay own a pair of those boots, whether they fish or not. I have a pair myself. They're good for slogging through mud."

"Oh." Faith's shoulders slumped in disappointment. She accepted her phone back from him. "Hold on." She tapped to the photos she had taken on the dock Thursday night. "Is this the same kind of print?"

"It's hard to tell." Tobin pulled off his wool watch cap and ran a hand through his thick blond hair. "The sole of the boot has the same pattern, but I'd guess there are only a few variations. And if they were both bought at the local hardware store, chances are most of the boots in town have the same pattern. Plus, we can't tell if they're the same size."

By the time Officer Tobin took a statement from Faith and drove away, it was definitely too late for her to make it to church. Faith texted Eileen to confirm their late lunch plans.

Faith mulled over the boot print. At the employee meeting Friday morning, a gentleman had given his seat to Faith. He worked at the private boat dock, so he might own a pair of rubber boots like that. If he wasn't the stalker, maybe he knew something about snoopy fishermen.

She changed into shoes more suitable for walking, grabbed a coat, and wrapped a scarf over her hair to save it from the breeze. "Watson, do you want to join me for a walk? You'll be cooped up indoors the rest of the day, I'm afraid."

The cat hopped down from his perch on the back of an easy chair and darted out the door. He followed Faith past the sleeping late fall gardens and around the manor toward the ocean.

The smell of the sea enticed with the promise of fish. Large fish, the cat hoped. He had overheard a visitor explain to a child that whales were not fish, but they were the right shape. The cat was certain they would be the right flavor too.

They hiked toward the cliffs and the stairs that led down to a sandy beach. His human walked past the steps. The cat followed dutifully, although he paused to pounce on dried leaves skittering across their path. It was best to keep his hunting skills honed for next spring.

They descended a steep slope composed of neat steps interspersed with a gravel path. Then they walked toward a building and a thing the humans called a dock, although it was a fraction of the size of the two in town.

His human slowed. She was learning from him to approach with caution, but her technique still needed some work.

He crouched low to the ground to show her the proper way.

Faith had never had a reason to come to the Castleton Manor boathouse before. The small boats were for the sole use of the Jaxon family. Guests and most employees were unaware the dock even existed. Still, this was the closest place Faith could imagine to find fishermen who might wear rubber boots and go tramping through the flower bed at her cottage.

The Jaxons never did anything halfway. The boathouse was small, but it was solidly built and impeccably maintained. The foundation was thick stone that she guessed could withstand a gale. The front of the boathouse opened through two doors facing the sea that reminded Faith of those on a garage. Both doors were lowered, but she could see how easily a boat might be moved from indoors to the sea outside.

Faith tried to remember those moments Thursday night after she saw the harpoon fly across the north dock. The man with the walrus mustache had disappeared. She had seen boot prints she now knew were made by a particular type of footwear favored by fishermen.

Had the man with the mustache been chasing the harpoon thrower, or had he been fleeing the scene of a crime in which he was complicit? Had the murderer escaped the north dock in a boat? Perhaps the killer had stolen the antique harpoon from the manor, taken a boat to the Lighthouse Bay dock, murdered Raymond, then returned the same way.

The boathouse and small dock seemed deserted. A quiet spot with no witnesses would be the perfect place to commit murder. On top of the cliff, through a thick growth of trees and bushes, stood a cottage. It would be nearly invisible when the foliage was filled out. Like the boathouse, it was a traditional New England style, with clapboard siding.

Faith and Watson walked a groomed path to the side door of the boathouse. She tried turning the door handle, but it was secured with a heavy padlock.

Watson trotted out on the short dock and sat, intently watching the sea.

Silly cat. He was probably hoping freshly baked tunaroons would leap out of the water and land at his feet.

Faith heard a scraping noise. She listened, then followed the sound to the back of the boathouse.

A man in a heavy canvas work jacket shoveled gravel from a wheelbarrow to the base of the small building. Unlike the costumed museum employee Faith had seen the night of the ship dedication, this man's black whiskers were probably real. He could have stepped out of a painting of an early 1800s whaling ship crew if not for the rubber boots. Faith was pretty sure those hadn't been invented until halfway through that century.

The man glanced up when she approached, leaned against the shovel, and pulled a bandanna from his pocket to wipe his brow. So much for her theory about the place being deserted, but he was precisely the person she had been hoping to find.

"Good morning. I'm Faith Newberry, the librarian at the manor."

"Glenn Dobie. Boathouse keeper. I'd offer to shake your hand, but I've been working." He held up one hand, covered with a soiled leather glove. "I remember you from the meeting the other morning. Sad deal."

"Yes," Faith agreed. "Terrible." She hesitated, debating how much to tell Glenn. Marlene had warned the staff not to discuss the death with guests. Faith decided it would be all right to talk to a fellow employee in the interest of solving Raymond's murder. "I was there when it happened."

"That must have been terrifying." Glenn's weathered face creased with concern. He didn't look at her as if she were a witness who needed to be eliminated.

"Thankfully, I didn't actually see it," Faith said. "But I saw a few boats moored to the north dock. The killer may have been trying to reach one of the boats to escape. Since the harpoon was stolen from the manor, I wondered if anyone might have taken a boat from here Thursday night."

Glenn shrugged. "We maintain only a few small craft, but it's under my purview, and I take my responsibilities seriously. I don't have a clear view of the boathouse from my cottage." He nodded toward the top of the cliff. "But I am careful to lock everything up tight when I'm not here."

Faith remembered the padlock. That would certainly make entering the boathouse difficult. She wondered whether the garage-style doors opening to the sea were locked. "Do you mind if I ask a few questions?"

"I don't see why not."

Faith wanted to ask whether Glenn had been stumbling around in her flower garden, but she decided a head-on confrontation might be a poor approach. Especially when her only backup was a cat. "Could someone take a boat from this dock to the ones in Lighthouse Bay?"

"The police already asked," Glenn answered. "Yes, it's entirely possible. It's done frequently in the summer. But the weather was foul Thursday night. Besides, guests aren't allowed to use the boats. Some liability issue or other."

"Has anyone else taken a boat out lately?"

"No family members have taken a boat from here in several months. It hardly seems worth keeping the boathouse going, although I'm not complaining. I like my job. The Jaxons are generous folks, and living in the cottage is part of the deal."

"Yes, they are generous," Faith agreed. She stopped herself from mentioning that she lived in the gardener's cottage. If Glenn had been the person snooping around her house, he probably already knew where she lived. "Theoretically, could a person take a boat from here to Lighthouse Bay in spite of the weather?"

"Sure, but a person would be daft to have taken one of our small craft out in a snowstorm."

"Would you know if they did?"

"Only if they hadn't made it back. Then I would've noticed a boat missing. Everything's in its proper place." Glenn lifted another scoop full of gravel. "Except for this. That storm was mild by New England standards, but a patch of gravel got washed away from the foundation. It'll only deteriorate more as the weather turns worse this winter."

Faith nodded, trying to come up with another question.

"If you'll excuse me, I need to get back to work." He resumed filling the hole.

Faith turned to leave, but another thought struck her. "If a person took a motorboat, they would have used gas, right?"

"Yes, they would've." Lines creased his face as he obviously considered her question and its implications. "The police didn't ask me that, and I didn't think of it."

Score one for me.

Glenn stuck his shovel in the loose gravel pile and dusted his gloved hands together. "Let's go take a look-see."

Faith followed Glenn to the dockside of the boathouse, where he unlocked the heavy padlock and swung open the door.

As she stepped inside, Faith considered briefly that the boathouse keeper shoveled heavy gravel with ease. He would have no trouble overpowering her. If he meant her harm, she had just walked into a trap. But his attention was obviously elsewhere. She relaxed a little as she watched Glenn scan the interior of the small building.

Sunshine spilled through the doorway. The air inside was chilly, but Faith could detect the faint odors of gasoline, old wood, and briny seawater.

One wall was covered with orange life jackets, fishing gear, and tools. Sawhorse-style frames rested on a narrow section of concrete floor, with three canoes and two small rowboats resting across them, upside down. A larger boat cradled in canvas webbing hung from a crane next to the large doors that opened to the sea. Everything appeared neat and tidy.

On the landside wall, stands supported small outboard motors. A canoe or rowboat could only be used on the calmest days, Faith suspected. Today the waves were choppy. Thursday night had been worse. She touched the larger boat, noticing how easily the crane moved.

"Are those doors locked?" Faith pointed to the garage-style doors that opened to the sea.

"No need," Glenn said. "A person would have to stand in waist-deep seawater to lift the doors. So far, no one's been determined enough to steal these old boats to get their feet wet."

Glenn walked to a red plastic fourteen-gallon gas tank. Two wheels made it portable, and a small hose and pump enabled filling the motors.

Faith could see the convenience of a tank that could be rolled out on the dock to refill a motorboat. A clear strip of plastic molded into the side of the red tank showed golden fluid up to the twelve-gallon mark.

Glenn squatted beside the tank and studied the clear strip. He shook his head, then stood and twisted off the fuel cap. He pulled a small flashlight from his jacket pocket and peered inside. He replaced the cap, then scratched his head, rumpling his short black hair.

"Is something wrong?" Faith asked.

"I was certain the tank was topped off. I keep careful track because it's not easy hauling this tank to town for a refill. I usually bring gasoline down here a gallon or two at a time, rather than carry this up the steps to my truck." Glenn examined the motors, resting on their special frames. He twisted off the fuel caps, aiming the flashlight and one eye at each opening. "Hmm."

"What is it?" Faith asked.

"I always drain these tanks when I know they won't be used for a while." Glenn made motions with his hands, shooing Faith out of the boathouse. "The police told me to call them if I thought of something else. I'd better talk to them before telling tales that may have no bearing on the situation."

Faith was disappointed, but she had to get to work, and she could tell Glenn wasn't going to share his insight. Besides, she had a pretty good idea what he had discovered. Someone had taken a boat out, then carefully returned everything to its proper place. Except the person hadn't drained the motor or replenished the container of gas.

It seemed unlikely someone had access to the boathouse key. Glenn appeared to be a well-organized and cautious man.

Had the killer entered through the garage doors to the sea?

8

As Faith left the boathouse, she spotted Watson, still sitting at the end of the dock.

The cat abandoned his post when she called him and trotted beside her as she walked up the path, along the cliffs, and toward their cottage. The morning had warmed up.

After she traded her coat for a lighter jacket and her walking shoes for low heels, she fed Watson a tunaroon. The cat was not pleased to be left at home, and he voiced his complaint with tart mews.

Walking past the dormant manor gardens, Faith smelled the distinctive odor of the cedar hedge. Tall, thick, and green, even in winter, the aromatic trees surrounded the Peter Pan fountain. The fountain had been drained of water before the first freeze, but the statue of the boy who refused to grow up still drew guests with cameras.

Faith heard dry rustling behind the hedges, even though there was no breeze. "Hello?"

No one answered.

Surely a guest would acknowledge her greeting. Perhaps she had been foolish to share what she knew with the boathouse keeper. Glenn might not be planning to call the police. Maybe he had sent Faith away so he could follow her and eliminate a witness.

He didn't seem like a murderer. But neither did Tasi or Milton, and both guests had more reason to kill Raymond than Glenn did. Maybe one of them had tracked Faith's journey to the boathouse and realized she was close to discovering the truth.

And then there was the unknown man on the north dock with the walrus mustache. What was his role in the murder? Innocent bystander or participant?

Faith paused, listening. The rustling sounds stopped. *Squirrels must be digging up acorns they buried earlier in the season.* Convinced her imagination was getting the better of her, she continued toward the manor.

A bird burst out of the cedar hedge with a rush of wings.

Faith jumped, and a startled yelp escaped her lips. She laughed at her own reaction. It was just a bird. Not a killer.

Then she heard several steps slowly crunch across the paving stones surrounding the dry fountain. She froze. They were definitely human steps.

"Hello?" she called again. "Who's there?"

The noise stopped.

Certain now that she was being watched, she had two choices: make a run for the manor and safety, or confront the stalker. She turned toward the hedge. Faith debated whether it was wise to step behind the tall hedges to search for a killer when there didn't seem to be anyone else outdoors.

The crunching on paving stones began again, moving away from her. The person was retreating.

Curiosity propelled her closer. Gray fabric was visible behind a thin patch in the hedge. Stepping quickly through a neatly trimmed opening between the tall evergreen bushes, Faith saw only the statue of Peter Pan.

A bit of gray, perhaps the hem of a coat, disappeared into the maze.

Faith rushed around the fountain. She hesitated before following. Faith had been through the maze, and she was reasonably certain she wouldn't get lost. She raced along a straight section, then took the first left turn.

Her feet tangled with an object, and Faith nearly sprawled onto the gravel path. She grasped a handful of hedge at the last moment, saving herself from a tumble.

Faith stood still for a moment, catching her breath. She looked around but saw nothing she could have tripped over. Determined to find the stalker, she resumed a more cautious journey through the maze. The person must have been confident he or she had eluded her. Instead of stealthy movement, Faith heard loud footsteps coming from the other side of a hedge.

She rushed through an opening, more mindful of where she placed her feet this time. Faith landed in the middle of the path, her hands extended protectively in front of her.

A small dog yipped. Three guests gasped, no doubt surprised by Faith's sudden appearance.

"Did you see someone going this way?" Faith asked. Her abrupt question and her shortness of breath must have been as startling as her ridiculous leap into the center of the path.

The guests huddled together and stared.

One guest held the leash of the adorable white bichon frise that had yipped at Faith. The small dog looked like a teddy bear, with the thick fur framing its face trimmed into a puffy ball. The woman holding the leash wore an equally fluffy faux fur jacket. "Miss Newberry?" the woman asked.

"Yes." Faith adopted her best professional tone, as though she wasn't breathless from stalking a person who had been stalking her. "May I help you?"

The other dog walkers, a woman accompanied by a pug and a man with a boxer, seemed to relax.

"Thank goodness you came along just now," the man said.

Have they been threatened by a killer?

"We're quite hopelessly lost," the pug's owner admitted.

Oh, of course. Faith really was letting her imagination run wild.

"And no, we haven't seen anyone else in the maze," the woman holding the bichon frise's leash said, "or we would have followed them out."

"No one else in the maze?" Faith repeated.

The trio shook their heads in unison.

Faith might have been annoyed that they had prevented her from identifying a stalker and potential murder suspect, but on the other hand, they might have saved her from a dangerous confrontation.

"I would be happy to guide you out," Faith offered. "I'm on my way to the manor to open the library."

Fortunately, they didn't ask why she was rushing around the maze. Instead, they introduced themselves and made small talk about the conference as they walked.

The person with the pug spoke. "I'm looking forward to your talk Thursday morning."

"I'm happy to hear that," Faith said. "I'll be speaking at the same time as some other compelling presentations."

"I'd rather learn your thoughts on men's adventure novels versus women's literature of the era."

Faith laughed. "I'm not picking sides. The emphasis of this conference is on whaling literature, but during the same time frame as *Moby-Dick* and *Twenty Thousand Leagues Under the Sea*, gentler tales such as *Little Women* were published and created an interesting contrast."

Once they entered the manor, Faith chatted with the guests for a few more minutes, then excused herself to open the library. They had helped her more than they knew. She needed to leave the detective work to the police and focus on her talk.

Whoever had been following her was long gone. And maybe that was a good thing.

Faith tried without success to push thoughts of Raymond's demise from her mind while she assisted guests searching for books recommended by conference presenters. The murder investigation was in the capable hands of the Lighthouse Bay Police.

Glenn had said he was calling them with the information about missing gasoline. Unless he was the person who had stalked her through the garden, prepared to stop her from giving a vital clue to the police. But what motivation did the boathouse keeper have to kill Raymond?

The three guests she had rescued had not seen anyone else in the maze. The stalker's identity would have to remain a mystery for now.

Judith had claimed her husband was lured to the north dock by a scrimshander. The only reason Faith could imagine for a scrimshaw artist to murder Raymond was to steal the *Essex* piece.

Someone with access to the gallery had stolen the antique harpoon. Maybe the same person had "borrowed" a motorboat from the boathouse, traveled to Lighthouse Bay, murdered Raymond, then put the boat away before Glenn noticed.

In a snowstorm and choppy seas? Faith was grasping at straws. It was another reminder that she needed to leave police work to the experts.

The library was empty when Faith locked up around midafternoon. Most of the conference guests had left to attend a private tour of the replica whaling ship *Constance Merit*.

If Faith hurried, she could pick up a special treat for Watson to make up for locking him indoors on such a nice day, then enjoy a visit with her aunt at Snickerdoodles.

As she drove through Lighthouse Bay to Midge's Happy Tails Gourmet Bakery, Faith saw merchants and residents garbed in early 1800s attire. If a man wearing a walrus mustache murdered Raymond, there were plenty of suspects from which to choose.

Faith entered the pet bakery and noticed Tasi perusing the display case of cat treats. She carried her beloved Alika. Watson would be upset if he knew he'd missed seeing his new cat friend shopping in his favorite store.

Sarah Goodwin, the manager of Happy Tails, craned her neck to look around Faith. Her curly auburn ponytail fell across one shoulder. "Where's your handsome companion? I rarely see you without him."

"I told him he had to stay home today," Faith said. "And for once, I think he listened."

Tasi turned her gaze from the cat treats to Faith. "Is the tuxedo cat from the library your companion?" She resembled a college professor with her hair pulled back in a braided chignon, and she wore a suit that seemed bland compared to her usual colorful dresses. A wool coat in a pleasant gray pattern was probably a recent purchase that would remain in a closet in her Hawaiian home.

"Yes," Faith said. "And I'm afraid he has quite a crush on Alika."

"I'm not surprised," Sarah said to Tasi. "Your Persian is a real beauty. And Watson is known for his impeccable taste."

"Speaking of taste," Tasi said, "I'm overwhelmed by the selection. Faith, can you tell me which treats your Watson favors?"

"You can't go wrong with Midge's goodies," Faith said, "although he seems so intrigued by the paintings of whales in the manor that I'm sure he wishes Midge would create a new whale-flavored treat. The conference appears to have captured his imagination."

Tasi laughed.

A thought occurred to Faith. She hoped Tasi wouldn't think she was rude for prying. She had decided to leave the investigation of Raymond's murder to the police, but since she had just happened to run into Tasi, surely it couldn't hurt to ask a few questions. "Speaking of the conference, the manor was nearly empty when I left. Everyone had gone on the tour."

Tasi shook her head. "To tell the truth, I'm a little weary of crowds. I've seen restored whaling ships and sailed on outrigger canoes. I may tour the *Constance Merit* later after the crowd leaves."

Faith understood the need for quiet time. She glanced toward the counter. Sarah nodded as she answered a customer's question. Faith might not have another private moment with Tasi, especially when they returned to the conference.

"I was on the *Constance Merit* the night Mr. Prather died." Faith watched Tasi's expression.

Lines creased between the tall woman's eyes. Faith couldn't tell whether she was concerned or annoyed.

"As much as Alika and I are enjoying the conference, I thought surely Mrs. Prather would leave. She just lost her husband, yet it appears she and her sister will stay for the entire week."

Annoyed, Faith decided. Tasi definitely did not like the Prathers. Faith needed to be cautious. She didn't want to gossip, but she needed answers.

"Mrs. Prather might be in shock," Faith suggested. "Perhaps the reality of her loss hasn't sunk in yet. Or she might be staying at the conference in the hope that the *Essex* scrimshaw will be recovered."

Tasi smiled. "That's what I like about Lighthouse Bay. People here are so positive and optimistic, and you never seem to speak ill of others." Her expression turned somber. "Even so, a man was murdered Thursday night. A killer was in this town. Perhaps still is."

A chill ran up Faith's spine. Tasi was right. But was she merely speculating, or did she know for a fact that Raymond's killer was still in Lighthouse Bay?

9

Faith steeled herself and decided to risk both Marlene's wrath for discussing the murder with a guest and tipping off a murderer that she was on the trail.

"Judith told me Raymond was meeting a scrimshander on the north dock," Faith said. "I saw the man with him while I was searching for Watson. He had a mustache, like half the men in town this week. I couldn't understand why they would meet secretly."

Tasi was quiet for a moment. When she spoke, her voice was almost a whisper. "There might be a reason. If scrimshaw is carved on ivory, walrus tusk, or whalebone, it must be documented."

"To ensure that it's actually a historical piece?" Faith was thinking of the concerns about whether the *Essex* scrimshaw was authentic.

"Well, that too. But mainly because whales are protected by endangered species laws and international regulations. Ivory scrimshaw created before 1972 is legal to buy and trade across state lines in the United States, but you need the proper paperwork to prove its provenance. Walrus ivory is also regulated, and it can only be harvested by native Alaskan people."

"Are you saying Raymond may have been purchasing illegal scrimshaw?"

Tasi stroked Alika's snowy head. "I would never presume to know another collector's motivations or level of scrupulousness. But if I were making a purchase, I would not lurk around a dock at night."

"One last question," Faith said. "Do you think the *Essex* scrimshaw was real?"

Tasi shrugged. "The Prathers wouldn't let me or Mr. Waldrin see it. I would not venture a guess. It has gone missing, so we may never know. Now I have a question for you."

Faith prepared herself to be on the receiving end of inquisition.

Tasi stepped toward the treat case. "Which cat treat do you think my Alika would prefer?"

Faith smiled with relief. "Tunaroons are Watson's favorite, but he also likes shrimp whiskers."

Sarah had completed ringing up a sale and returned her attention to Tasi and Faith. "Why don't you let Alika decide?" Sarah suggested. She handed Tasi a sample of each.

Faith made her purchase, then left Tasi and Alika to the treat tasting. As Faith walked out of the store, she wondered whether Tasi could have killed Raymond, either as revenge for his insults about her expertise or to steal the *Essex* scrimshaw.

She shook her head. She could stew about it later. It was time to meet Eileen at Snickerdoodles.

Midafternoon was a good time to meet at the popular bakery. Snickerdoodles was relatively quiet at this time of day.

Eileen was already waiting inside. Faith only hoped she looked as youthful as her aunt when she reached her sixties. Eileen's brown hair was pulled back loosely with a clip. She wore a calf-length suede skirt, knee-high boots, and a soft cardigan she had knitted with a pattern of oak leaves in muted autumn colors.

They ordered, then sat down at a small table in the corner. Faith was able to bring Eileen up to speed without fear of being overheard by half the town.

As Faith filled her in about the boot print in her flower bed and her conversation with Glenn at the boathouse, Eileen listened attentively, glancing down occasionally at her knitting or pausing to take a sip of tea or a bite of sandwich.

Faith didn't want to worry Eileen more than she already was, so she decided not to mention the stalker in the garden. Besides, it sounded ridiculous. Instead, she told her aunt about her conversation with Tasi moments before.

Eileen tucked her knitting into her bag. "Do you have to return to work right away?"

Faith checked her watch. "I have an hour before I have to reopen the library."

"I think we should ask someone about scrimshaw who doesn't appear to be involved in Raymond's death."

"Who is that?"

"Corrie Baker sells scrimshaw in her antique shop."

"Great idea. I could ask her about the receipt I saw on the dock too."

Faith and Eileen left the bakery and walked to The Fishwife's Attic. They wandered around for a few minutes until Corrie had completed a transaction with a customer.

"Nice to see you ladies," Corrie said, smiling. "Are you looking for something in particular?"

The solution to Raymond Prather's murder, Faith thought. She had to be careful what she said. She didn't want to encourage idle gossip. What she needed were facts.

"I see you have scrimshaw art." Eileen gestured toward the neat rows of gleaming pieces in a glass display case. "I'm surprised they're so affordable."

"These are replicas of historical scrimshaw," Corrie explained. "They're carved on cow bone or man-made materials, not ivory."

"That must be what the decor in my cottage is," Faith said. "I can't imagine the Jaxons placing valuable—and portable—art in their employee's living quarters."

"I'm careful to let customers know what they're buying," Corrie continued. "Real scrimshaw pieces, especially historically significant ones, are out of most casual tourists' price range."

"I suppose it's like buying a print instead of an original painting," Eileen said. "A less expensive copy of art."

Corrie nodded. "Like my faux Tiffany lamps. A person might

like the look but can't afford the real thing. As long as you know it's a replica, of course. I would never mislead someone."

But not everyone was as scrupulous as Corrie Baker.

Faith scrolled through the photos on her cell phone until she came to the receipt she had seen on the north dock. The Fishwife's Attic logo was clearly displayed. "Can you tell me who made this purchase?" She showed Corrie the picture.

Corrie studied it, then put a hand over her heart. "Oh, that was just terrible! Poor Mr. Prather had been in my shop earlier that day. I had no idea that would be the first and last time I would ever see him."

"What did he purchase?" Faith pressed.

"The police asked the same question." Corrie stepped behind the counter. "The Fishwife's Attic may be an antique shop, but I use modern means to manage the business." She tapped a few keys on her computer keyboard. "Yes, Thursday afternoon Mr. Prather bought a scrimshaw replica."

So Raymond had bought scrimshaw. He must have been the one to drop the receipt on the dock.

Corrie opened the case and retrieved an object. "It was like this but with a slightly different ship."

Apparently, replica scrimshaw did not need the careful handling the real thing required. Faith took the piece from Corrie and turned it around, studying it from all angles. How did the experts determine what was historical and what was modern? She couldn't tell.

"Why would a serious collector buy a scrimshaw replica?" Eileen asked.

"Mr. Prather said he was giving it to his nephew," Corrie answered. "He was going to the young man's birthday party this coming Wednesday. It just breaks my heart to think of Mr. Prather's poor wife."

Faith glanced at her aunt, hoping Corrie's words didn't affect her.

Eileen had lost her husband far too young, but she had carried on with her life with her trademark positive attitude.

"Another guest from the manor visited me that day," Corrie said, "but she didn't purchase anything."

"Who was that?" Faith blurted out.

Eileen raised one eyebrow, signaling that Faith's approach had been a bit abrupt.

"A tall woman wearing a long dress covered with bright flowers. She carried a beautiful white cat."

Tasi Kekoa. Faith's heart beat faster. Tasi had the motivation to kill Raymond, and she had been in Lighthouse Bay Thursday evening. "What time was she here?" Faith asked.

"I remember I had the shop open later than usual that night," Corrie replied, "because there were people in town for the ship dedication. I locked the doors right after she left at seven."

That was a half hour before Faith had checked her watch on the *Constance Merit*. She had rushed to the north dock when she spotted Watson. Tasi could have run the few blocks to the dock but not with a cat and a harpoon in her arms. It was possible she'd stolen the antique harpoon from the gallery, shopped at The Fishwife's Attic, left Alika in her rental car if she had one, then gone to the dock to murder Raymond. The timing sounded right.

At the thought of time, Faith glanced at her watch. "I didn't realize it was this late. I need to get back to work."

They thanked Corrie for the information and said their goodbyes.

Eileen walked with Faith to her car. "Don't forget our book club meeting tonight."

"I wouldn't miss it for the world," Faith said. "I need something to take my mind off the conference. This is so sad. Raymond may have been murdered for fake scrimshaw."

"We don't know that's what happened," Eileen reminded her. "Why was Raymond on the dock in the first place?"

"From what Tasi said, he might have been buying illegal scrimshaw."

"What did replica and illegal scrimshaw have to do with Raymond's death?"

"Maybe nothing," Faith said. "Maybe everything."

Faith checked on Watson in the cottage briefly, trying to appease him with a treat. Strangely, he didn't seem upset to have been locked up all day.

"I promise I'll take you to the book club meeting tonight," Faith told the cat.

He blinked slowly, the signal Faith imagined meant approval or agreement.

She arrived just minutes before the conference attendees returned from their tour of the *Constance Merit*.

When people entered the library, they were excited to view Angus Jaxon's log and relics that had been referred to during their ship tour. Faith was too busy the rest of the afternoon to think about all the new information she had accumulated.

Finally, the workday ended, and Faith locked up. She had a quick dinner at home, then grabbed her copy of *The Little Women Letters* by Gabrielle Donnelly, a modern take on Louisa May Alcott's classic.

Watson followed her to the car, and she drove to the Candle House Library, a building once used for candle manufacturing that now housed a public library within its stone walls.

When Faith and Watson entered the main room, they found Eileen, Brooke, and Midge already settled into the comfy reading chairs surrounding the massive fireplace. While the library at the manor was luxurious, the Candle House Library leaned more toward comfortable.

Faith took a seat next to Midge and reached out to pet the Chihuahua in her friend's lap. Atticus was a regular at the book club meetings. Tonight the dog wore a tiny sweater, but he still seemed to crave sitting close to the fireplace. His toenails and Midge's manicured nails were painted with the same fuchsia polish.

Watson ignored the little dog and curled up on the floor in front of the cozy fire.

After discussing the novel, Midge requested an update on Raymond's murder. "I feel out of the loop. You gals have been in the thick of the investigation." She was originally from Alabama, and she still retained a slight Southern accent.

"It's not exactly an investigation," Faith clarified.

Eileen took out her current knitting project and set to work. "I disagree. We made progress today, and Faith discovered an important clue this morning."

The ladies perched on the edge of their seats as Faith told them about the boathouse keeper and his concern that a boat may have been taken out without permission.

"How could a motorboat leave the dock without Glenn noticing?" Midge asked.

"His cottage is above the boathouse on top of the cliff," Faith replied. "And it's surrounded by trees. They may have no leaves this time of year, but I can believe he might not hear a motorboat leaving and returning."

"Especially that night." Brooke shivered despite her sparkly pink sweater. "I nearly froze on the dock."

"What does that mean?" Midge asked. "Did the murderer come from the manor?" She held on to Atticus with both hands, as though protecting the tiny dog.

"I believe the antique harpoon that was stolen from the gallery is the weapon I saw used to murder Raymond," Faith said, "although the police won't confirm my theory. The killer must have taken it from the manor Thursday night before going to Lighthouse Bay. What better way to sneak onto the north dock than from the sea?"

"Also, Faith spoke to Tasi Kekoa this afternoon." Eileen glanced up from her knitting. "She was shopping in The Fishwife's Attic shortly before the murder. But Corrie didn't mention that Tasi was soaked, as she would have been had she motored a boat across choppy seas to Lighthouse Bay."

"Good point," Faith agreed. "Plus, Corrie said Tasi had Alika when she was in the antique shop. I can't imagine that lovely Persian cat getting her fur wet."

"But maybe the manor's boat dock and the mystery of the missing gasoline is just a red herring," Brooke suggested.

Watson stared at the young woman, his green eyes opening wide.

Brooke shook a scolding finger at the cat. "Not all fish are for eating. Especially my Diva and Bling, so don't get any ideas. A red herring is a false clue in a mystery, not a snack for you."

"You're right about the red herring," Faith said. "It occurred to me that Tasi could have driven to town with the harpoon. She didn't need to break into the boathouse to steal a boat in order to reach the north dock."

"How many guests even know about the private dock?" Brooke asked. "I've worked at the manor for years, and I just learned it existed."

"Someone hiking around could run into it," Faith said.

"Someone walking a dog." Eileen paused in her knitting. "Like Milton Waldrin."

"Not Milton," Brooke objected. "He's too nice, and his little dog couldn't hike that far on its short legs."

"Dachshunds are working dogs," Eileen said. "They may be short, but they're powerfully built."

"I hope Milton's not the killer," Brooke said. "I'm going to dinner with him Wednesday night."

Faith found it hard to believe the shy man could work up the nerve to ask a woman on a date, especially a much younger woman.

"Who is this Milton guy?" Midge asked Brooke. "And if you think he might be a killer, why on earth would you go to dinner with him?"

"Whether he's dangerous or not," Eileen said, "it's a bad idea to go out with a guest. There must be some rule against it."

"This isn't a date," Brooke said. "Milton wants to thank me for saving Boomer from nearly taking a spill down the manor's front steps. He said the dog could have been severely hurt. Dachshunds might be sturdy, but their backs are delicate. Besides, I was planning to ask Faith to come along as a chaperone." She turned to Faith. "What do you think?"

Put on the spot, Faith didn't know how to respond. "Well, I don't think it's a good idea to go alone. If we can ask Milton a few subtle questions, maybe we could eliminate him as a murder suspect."

"Just for the record, I don't approve." Eileen looked from Faith to Brooke. "I know you two are grown women and will do what you want, but I think it's inappropriate."

Brooke lowered her head, her shoulders slumped. "Maybe we should rethink the plan."

The discussion drifted to the happier topics of Eileen's grandchildren, Midge's son and daughter, and everyone's plans for the upcoming Thanksgiving holiday.

The book club ended amicably, and the women put on their coats, hats, and gloves so they could brave the chilly evening.

But when Brooke asked Faith and Watson to walk her to her car, Faith knew something was up.

Brooke stopped beside her sporty red car. "I still think I should go to dinner with Milton," she whispered, even though there wasn't another soul in sight. "I don't think he's the murderer."

"We don't know that for sure," Faith whispered back.

"I wish I could bring Diva and Bling to the manor, like you bring Watson with you to work. My angelfish could warn me if Milton is dangerous."

Brooke thought her two angelfish could spot a loser. She claimed they swam around their tank in a frenzy, signaling to their owner if a potential romantic interest was bad news. Now it sounded like she believed they could detect criminals too.

"You wouldn't want your fish in the manor kitchen." Faith smiled. "Terrible things could happen."

"You're not implying they could become sushi, are you?" Brooke turned to her car, then pulled a piece of paper from beneath the windshield wiper. "It shouldn't be a parking ticket. I made sure I was in a legal space."

As Brooke unfolded the paper, Faith tried to read over her shoulder. It looked like Watson craned his neck as if to see the note too. Which was a silly idea, because Faith was certain her cat couldn't read. Pretty sure, anyway.

"'Ignorance is the parent of fear,'" Brooke read out loud.

"It's a quote from *Moby-Dick*."

"The rest of the note is the scary part." Brooke continued, "'Quit snooping. You're better off afraid than dead.'"

Brooke and Faith stared at each other for a moment.

"That's crazy," Brooke said. "I haven't done any sleuthing. Not as much as you."

"Maybe the person has us confused and thought this was my car." Faith reached for the note, holding it delicately by one corner. "It's a good thing we're both wearing gloves. The police can check it for fingerprints. I think we need to take it to the station right now."

The cat was not happy when his human locked him inside the car. He might miss something important. Humans lacked the intuitive detecting skills of felines, and they often let the obvious slip right by them.

When his human finally climbed back inside the car, bringing a big dose of night chill with her, she seemed pensive. He tried meowing once to indicate that she should talk to him, but she didn't take the hint.

They rode to the cottage in silence. She parked, then opened the passenger door for him.

He smelled something on the breeze. The same something he'd smelled on the north dock in Lighthouse Bay.

When his human reached for him, he used a tried-and-true evasive maneuver.

His human called for him to come back.

He glanced over his shoulder, waited for her to approach, then took off again. She would figure it out. This was no ordinary game of "catch me if you can."

The night was too cold to chase a cat across the expansive Castleton Manor grounds, but it was also too cold to allow Watson to spend the night outside. Faith did not have the energy to sit up waiting for Watson to mew at the front door or tap on a window from his perch on the sill.

She took a small flashlight out of her purse. The light was more suited for locating the keyhole in the front door when she'd forgotten to leave the porch light on, but it did help her keep track of Watson. The white patches of his tuxedo markings reflected the light while his black fur blended with the dark.

Watson darted across grass crusty with frost.

Faith followed, sticking to the walking paths, where she was less likely to stumble.

The cat stopped, sniffed the air, turned to make sure she was coming, then continued on. He seemed headed for the ocean cliffs.

"You chose an inconvenient time of year to become fascinated with the ocean," Faith muttered more to herself than Watson.

His determined movements put more distance between them. At the top of the cliffs, he turned left, following the same path they'd used to reach the boathouse.

Faith halted and turned off her flashlight. Her heart rate, already elevated from the late-night hike, increased still more.

Below them, bumping along a path behind the boathouse, was a hooded figure. A wheelbarrow trundled noisily, bouncing and threatening to overturn on the uneven ground. Whoever it was appeared too thin to be Glenn, but distance could mar her perception.

Why would the boathouse keeper be working outside at night in the dark when he could turn on the lights lining the eaves of the building and running down the dock?

Watson stopped abruptly in the middle of the path.

The person with the wheelbarrow glanced around.

Faith squatted beside Watson, hoping the leafless branches of the bushes lining the path would conceal her. In the dark, she couldn't tell who it was, but she could tell who it wasn't. Unless Glenn had shaved off his whiskers and lost weight suddenly, that was not him.

Faith debated what to do. Climb the steep steps to Glenn's cottage? She would risk being seen by the stranger with the wheelbarrow. She wished she had thought to get Glenn's telephone number, so she could call and warn him.

Instead, she followed Watson's cue and remained hidden in the bushes. Although the day had been pleasant, the temperature had cooled significantly with the setting sun. Faith shivered, but she was determined to stay. Eventually, the person had to climb the path up the cliff, head for Glenn's cottage, or leave in a boat.

She couldn't tell what the person was doing, but anyone sneaking around in the dark had to be up to no good.

Faith remembered that Officer Tobin had scolded her for not calling the police immediately when she had heard someone walking around her cottage the night before. She reached in her purse, fumbled around for her cell phone, and dialed the Lighthouse Bay police. She reached Officer Rooney this time, and she explained in whispers where she was and what she was doing.

"I can barely hear you," Rooney said. "But from what I understand, I suggest you get to the nearest safe place and let us handle it."

"I'm worried about Mr. Dobie."

"There's a road to his cottage. Officer Tobin is on patrol. He'll be there soon."

As Faith wondered if it would be better to wait for the police to arrive, Watson headed back up the walking path. Faith followed. Several times the cat dashed ahead, then stopped to wait for Faith to catch up.

When they reached the house, Faith's hands were trembling with cold and adrenaline, making it difficult to unlock the door.

Watson mewed with impatience.

"I'm cold too, Rumpy. I'll freeze out here before I get the door unlocked." Her hands finally steadied for a moment, and Faith opened the door.

Watson slipped past her feet and shot inside.

Faith warmed up with a cup of hot tea. She huddled in an easy chair, covering her lap with her grandmother's quilt. Watson curled up on her lap. Faith wouldn't have imagined she could doze off after the earlier excitement, but when her phone rang, she jumped. Watson nearly spilled off her lap.

Faith grabbed the phone and answered.

"This is Officer Tobin. May I ask you a few questions?" Patrolling at night must have made him forget that regular folks were normally asleep at this hour.

"I'm still sitting up." Which wasn't exactly a fib. She wasn't completely awake, but she hadn't put on her pajamas and gone to bed either.

"I was hoping you were available. I prefer taking statements in person. I'm in the driveway. Do you mind if I come in?"

Faith tried to shake the rest of the fuzz out of her head as she opened the door.

Officer Mick Tobin appeared alert, his uniform crisply pressed and his blond hair neatly combed.

Faith invited him into the kitchen for a cup of hot tea. He gladly accepted.

"Officer Rooney relayed to me what you told her over the phone," Tobin said. "I'd just like to clear up a few details. Why were you outside hiking in the dark?"

"I was chasing my cat."

As if to verify the story, Watson hopped up on a kitchen chair next to Tobin.

"I see. And Watson decided a midnight raid on the boathouse was in order?"

"He's been obsessed with the ocean ever since this conference started." Faith wanted to tell him that she suspected Watson had heard tales of Moby Dick and was trying to catch a whale, but she didn't want to sound silly. "We came back from a book club meeting. When I opened the car door, Watson took off."

Officer Tobin jotted down notes. "But you didn't hike all the way to the boathouse?"

"No. I stopped when I saw the person with a wheelbarrow. Did you catch them?"

"There was no one around. No wheelbarrow either. Of course, it was hard to search in the dark. I probably shouldn't tell you this, but Mr. Dobie came down with me. He didn't notice anything missing or disturbed. He thought maybe it was a fisherman."

"In the dark? And why did the person have a wheelbarrow?"

"Maybe they were hoping to catch Moby Dick."

Faith laughed. "They'd need something larger than a wheelbarrow."

Monday morning, Faith fixed a hot breakfast for herself and fed Watson. She still felt chilled, even after a hot shower and a cozy night's sleep under a heavy quilt. Well, not an entire night. She had spent some of it tossing and turning.

When she pulled on her coat, Watson trotted out of the kitchen to follow.

"Not today. I'm sorry, but you have to stay home again. Agnes raised a fuss with Marlene, and you can't come to the manor until the conference ends."

Not that Watson could be kept locked up. He had a way of moving through closed doors and secret passages without being detected. Still, he let Faith get out the door and lock the cottage without trying to escape. It seemed too easy.

The morning flowed in an easy rhythm of calm followed by hectic crowds as conference attendees flooded the library for the fifteen minutes between sessions. Often the guests came to see a book or an item in a display case that had been mentioned by a speaker.

A few people took a break from sessions to relax in the chairs in front of the fireplace. Naturally, whaling-era history and novels dominated the reading choices.

During her downtime, Faith pulled up her notes for her Thursday presentation, tweaking the slides and double-checking her dates and quotes. In the 1800s, many adventurous stories were written by men, but it was also the era of Jane Austen and her contemporaries.

Faith easily managed the library on her own, but around noon Laura dropped by.

"Do you need anything?" Laura asked Faith. "I'm on my lunch break, but I'd rather be here in the library than sitting in the break room. Besides, Brooke was using me as a taster in the kitchen, so I'm too full to eat the lunch I brought."

The manor had a nice employee break room, better than most Faith had seen, but she understood her librarian protégé wanting to spend every minute she could among the stacks of carefully curated books. "Would you mind watching the library for a little while?"

Laura smiled. "It would be my pleasure."

"I didn't bring my lunch, so I need to dash home and grab a bite to eat. It shouldn't be too busy here. Most of the guests are watching a movie in the salon."

Laura nodded. "First you should visit Brooke in the corridor outside the salon. If you're lucky, she might need a second opinion on the mini quiche she's serving during the movie intermission. It's delicious."

Faith left the library and walked through the gallery.

Vendors were lounging, but they sat at attention as soon as they saw Faith. When they recognized her, they went back to their crossword puzzles or smartphones.

She slowed when she saw the woman with the ivory hair comb.

"Have you come back for the comb?" the cheery vendor asked.

Faith considered and finally made herself read the price tag. The number was reasonable for such an extraordinary piece, but it was way outside her price range. "I've never seen anything like it, but I still have to take a pass."

"A pity. It's gorgeous against your auburn hair. I'm afraid Mr. Jaxon has his eye on it too."

As a gift for his mother. Faith reluctantly gave up her dream of a whale ivory comb. She walked past other vendor tables, determined to focus on her immediate task of getting lunch.

When she spied the vendor with the brown walrus mustache, she stopped. The mustache wasn't what caught her eye. Half the men in Lighthouse Bay wore a pasted-on mustache in that old-fashioned style. However, this man's mustache was real, and he was leaning over a small worktable, whittling on a piece of bone with a viciously sharp knife.

With a jolt, Faith realized he was a scrimshander.

11

Faith tried to still her shaking hand as she plucked a business card from a cast-iron card holder in the shape of a ship. *Owen Chase*, the card read. *Specializing in scrimshaw art and whaling-era antiquities.*

Could Owen be the man Raymond had met on the north dock? And if he was, had he seen Faith? Did he realize she was a witness to the murder?

Faith leaned toward the table to examine a piece of scrimshaw carved with a whimsical dolphin in an obviously modern style. "Excuse me. Did you design this?"

"That's not one of mine. I did these here." He waved a hand at a locked case without looking up at Faith.

The carving on the scrimshaw pieces was precise and detailed, mostly of old-fashioned ships with multiple square sails filled with wind. Next to one piece was an award ribbon.

"Those are amazing," Faith said. "How do you get those tiny ropes carved so beautifully?"

"Years of practice," Owen said, his words clipped. "And study. It's an art." He focused on the carving in his hand.

"I saw replica scrimshaw at a shop in town. Your work—"

Owen dropped his carving tool on the marble floor with a clatter. He ducked under the cloth-covered table to retrieve it, taking his sweet time.

She had been preparing to pay him a compliment. After seeing the replicas in The Fishwife's Attic, she realized Owen's work was of very high quality.

Owen finally straightened, glanced at Faith, then turned his back toward her as he wiped his sharp tool on a cloth.

Faith felt annoyed to be ignored until she considered that Owen might not be reacting out of mere avoidance of a person who clearly had no intention of making a purchase. He seemed afraid.

"I'll be on my way," Faith said.

Really, she should have just turned and left, but it wasn't her nature to be rude to people. She had to cut the man some slack. There were any number of reasons why Owen had avoided talking to her. If he really was the man who had been on the dock, maybe the police had asked him not to spread tales. Or he might have been deeply upset by witnessing a murder.

Then again, he could have stolen the *Essex* scrimshaw, either before or after Raymond was speared with a harpoon. Perhaps Faith had gotten it all wrong and the man with the walrus mustache hadn't been the one standing next to Raymond. Maybe he was the killer.

She hurried to the corridor outside the salon. Elegant vases containing flower arrangements decorated marble pedestals. Between them sat a long table. Brooke pushed a wheeled cart through one doorway as Faith entered through the other. Silver cloches covered trays of food.

Brooke smiled at her. "Great timing. You can snitch a taste before I arrange everything." She lifted a cloche.

A delicious smell wafted up to Faith, making her realize how hungry she was. "Are you sure it won't be missed?"

Brooke laughed. "Some guests are complaining that we feed them too well. As if I'm to blame if they overeat and gain a few pounds while on a literary retreat here. But I'm guessing these will go fast." She slid a serving spatula under a mini quiche and set it on a plate for Faith.

She grabbed a fork and took a bite. She closed her eyes as the flaky crust and savory filling melted in her mouth. "You've done it again. This is absolute perfection."

Brooke glanced at her watch. "The intermission begins in ten minutes. I'd better get the table set up before guests start coming out here."

"May I help?" Faith asked.

"Absolutely. Here's a pair of gloves."

Faith pulled on plastic serving gloves and followed Brooke's instructions for displaying the food and arranging serving utensils and dishes. The delicious food would be served on quality china and stainless steel flatware.

They were almost finished when Milton and Boomer entered the corridor. Both wore matching red bow ties and gray wool coats.

Faith stared. Gray wool. Like the coat she had glimpsed in the maze.

"Captain Boomer couldn't make it through to intermission," Milton explained. "We had to make a little trip to the doggy restroom."

"His coat is darling," Brooke said. "And it matches yours."

A blush reddened Milton's cheeks, already rosy from the November chill.

Boomer sat, his tongue hanging out, and wagged his tail. He seemed comfortable around people he knew. People who didn't try to hit him with walking canes.

"My sister enjoys sewing," Milton said. "She designs all of Boomer's outfits. He needs coats and sweaters with his short fur. He has hardly any undercoat."

Faith crouched down. She pulled a serving glove off and held her hand out to the dachshund. He gave her hand a quick lick. She patted his coat, which was cold from the outdoor air. As she straightened, she caught a glimpse of black-and-white fur flashing by, headed for one of the grand staircases. *No, it can't be Watson.*

"I need to finish up," Brooke said. "Faith, by the time you wash your hands, I'll be done. No offense, Captain Boomer."

"He understands." Milton surveyed the table loaded with treats. "I don't want to disturb the movie if it's almost intermission. I'm proud of how well Boomer has behaved. I thought the movie would be too frightening for him."

"You should get yourself a plate," Brooke said. "And there are some puppy-friendly treats from Happy Tails in the special dish with paw prints."

"Try the quiche," Faith told him. "It's delicious."

Guests emerged from the salon, blinking as their eyes adjusted from being in a dark room.

Faith watched to see if anyone else wore a gray coat. Gray was a good color to wear when skulking around dormant flower gardens. But the guests had all been indoors, watching the movie. Many wore sweaters and light jackets, but none had coats suitable for outdoors.

After Faith greeted a few guests, she said goodbye to Brooke and Milton. Then she walked toward the Great Hall, ready to relieve Laura.

She hadn't even made it to the gallery when a woman screamed.

Faith, along with guests and other staff members, rushed into the lobby.

Judith stood at the top of the stairs. "It wasn't enough for someone to steal my *Essex* scrimshaw. Now my entire collection is gone!"

Judith did not seem shocked as much as furious. As well she should be. How could a thief be so cruel as to rob the recent widow not just once but twice?

Marlene appeared, always prepared to handle a crisis. As she assessed the situation, her professional appearance and commanding presence seemed to calm the guests.

Faith decided this wasn't her business or her battle, so she helped Brooke herd guests back toward the salon. The second half of the movie would begin soon. Faith once again headed for the library, grateful to return to her haven.

Judith's scream had been loud enough to be heard all the way to the library, and Laura was anxious to learn what had happened. Faith filled her in, trying to convey information without gossiping.

"I'm glad you're so dedicated that you stayed in the library," Faith said. "There's nothing any of us can do for Judith. It's better to let the police handle it."

The human screamed. He knew her noise might draw attention to him, so the cat crouched down behind the stair railing. Lacking most of a tail had its advantages, as he had noticed how many cats thought they were hidden while their tails twitched and flicked, revealing their location.

He understood that his human wanted him to stay home, but an inquisitive fellow such as he would languish without activity. He had his secret ways of escaping the cottage, and he had nipped inside the manor behind his new friend, who was half a dog tall and a dog and a half long.

The woman had all the attention focused on her, so the cat trotted down the second-floor corridor. He sniffed until he discovered the lovely white Persian's scent, even though her delicate feet seemed never to touch the floor. The door to her room was closed.

The cat stuck his paw under the door, prodding and pulling, but the door would not budge. He risked a soft mew, hoping the Persian would come visit with him.

He heard a soft thud. The cat peeked under the door and spotted white paws and a pink nose.

Then he noticed a human topping the stairs and marching down the corridor. The cat had to flee or risk detection. There was no way for him to explain his extended absence from the manor, but at least now the Persian knew he had sought her out.

As the cat raced down the hall, he noticed a door standing open. Curious, he ducked inside.

Despite Marlene's best efforts to squelch gossiping among the manor employees, news reached Faith later that afternoon. She took the information with a grain of salt. Well, several grains.

Supposedly, although Judith had demanded every guest room and conference attendee be searched for her missing scrimshaw collection, the police had insisted there was only so much they could do. While they took statements, Marlene ran interference, trying to salvage the reputation of the manor and placate nervous guests.

With the theft of the harpoon, the *Essex* scrimshaw, and now the rest of the Prather collection, Faith decided she should focus on guarding the other collections on display in the library.

When she finished her day, Faith gathered her belongings and headed for the cottage.

On the way, Watson bounded up to her.

"How did you get out?" Faith asked the cat. "Have you been outside all day?"

She shivered as she hurried to open the front door. Faith checked the doors and windows, concerned that maybe someone had gotten in, thus letting Watson escape. Everything appeared secure and just as she had left it. *How does he do it?*

Watson had seemed to walk through locked doors before and found secret passages in the manor. She would have to search the cottage. If there was a place large enough for a cat to escape, a cat-size creature could get in.

Faith was too wrung out to do anything about that tonight. She barely had the energy to fix dinner, shower, and crawl into bed.

Before going to the library Tuesday morning, Faith decided to look up information about manor guests to see if anyone had a criminal record for theft. Her experience as a librarian and researcher often came in handy when a mystery was afoot.

She examined the business card she had gotten from Owen Chase. His website was colorful and informative. Owen specialized in scrimshaw art and whaling-era antiques. He had even won many prizes for his scrimshaw art in the New England area and as far away as Alaska.

Faith wondered how a person could make a living in such a specialized field. But then she saw that he also worked part-time in a museum and was a costumed interpreter at a Rhode Island living history museum during the summer. The man's career gave him easy access to antiques, but surely the museums would have noticed if he had stolen items.

The only thing unusual about Owen was that she suspected he was using an alias. Owen Chase was the name of the first mate of the ill-fated whaling ship *Essex*. Her heart beat faster as she dug into why a man would use a fake name, but she couldn't pinpoint a definite reason. Maybe it was a kind of gimmick related to his art and perfectly harmless.

Owen's name didn't come up in any articles about arrest, mayhem, or murder. Not that Faith had access to anything but the most public sorts of reporting. Still, it seemed like information on serious crimes would have shown up in an Internet search.

After all, she couldn't imagine that he would have gotten a job at the museum with a fake name. Unless he had changed his identity legally in an attempt to hide a criminal past. Maybe he'd chosen that name because it had historical significance and he knew it would increase his likelihood of landing historical jobs.

She pulled her mind out of its tailspin and checked into Tasi and Milton. Both were who they claimed to be, as confirmed by photographs and backgrounds. Of course, that did not remove either from the suspect list, but she didn't notice any red flags popping up.

It finally got interesting—but not for the reasons she expected—when she did an Internet search for Raymond and Judith Prather. Raymond had been on a career track as a stockbroker when he suddenly retired around the time he married Judith.

That might have seemed odd, but Judith's family was wealthy, their names and photos splashed across society pages. Perhaps after marrying Judith, Raymond didn't need to work. He could focus on managing his wife's considerable fortune.

Faith sat back. Something didn't add up. How could the *Essex* scrimshaw have required Judith's savings to purchase? She was a millionaire. Or had been.

Faith glanced at the clock. She would have to leave soon.

She looked up Agnes VanStuth. As a young woman, Agnes had been an Olympic hopeful, expected to make the track-and-field team easily. Agnes and her team had been en route to the qualifying trials when the bus crashed, breaking both her legs and ending her Olympic dreams.

How awful.

Faith shut down her computer and hurried to get ready for work.

Watson appeared at her feet, clearly ready for a day in the library.

Faith knelt and rubbed his neck. "I'm sorry, but we're only halfway through the conference. Marlene wants you to stay out of the manor until Agnes is gone. It's for your own safety. I don't want her to hurt you with that cane of hers."

Watson blinked slowly, as though he understood.

"Not that I can keep you locked up." Faith paid particular attention to the fact that Watson was inside as she closed and locked the door.

The cat waited the length of time required to groom himself from head to toe before exiting the cottage through his secret escape route. Castleton Manor might have intentionally created secret passages, but the old gardener's cottage had its own gaps that its renovation had failed to seal entirely.

The cat wriggled out into sunshine. He took a moment to clean the cobwebs from his whiskers, then scampered to the manor. He didn't need to sneak in. Humans were constantly coming and going. All he had to do was wait for an open door.

12

Faith was busy all morning, answering questions and assisting guests with research using the library's impressive collection of whaling-era literature, maps, and copies of ship's logs. Around noon, the entire manor became quiet as guests went to Lighthouse Bay for a tour of the historic town and a special presentation at the whaling museum.

Faith was shelving books when Brooke appeared, carrying two white boxes.

"We made box lunches for the guests," Brooke said, "but most people opted for lunch at The Captain's Table." The upscale restaurant had a view of the historic lighthouse and a reputation for excellent seafood.

"I would too if I didn't know what a fabulous box lunch the kitchen packs."

"The staff took the leftover lunches, and I snagged one for you." Brooke handed a box to Faith.

"Thank you. I was going to the cottage to check on Watson, but he'd probably just escape when I opened the door. Marlene has banished him from the manor until Agnes is gone. Watson almost tripped her."

"Agnes is not having a good time here," Brooke said.

Faith glanced around the expansive, two-story library. "We shouldn't talk about guests," she said, her voice lowered.

"Not here," Brooke said. "It's nice outside. Let's go for a walk."

Faith almost didn't need her coat. The weather had warmed to the midfifties, leaving patches of snow only in shaded areas. As they walked, Faith updated Brooke on her research and Agnes's sad denial of a chance to be in the Olympics.

"That still doesn't excuse her deliberately trying to hit Boomer with her cane."

"I was there," Faith said. "I'm not absolutely certain she meant to hit Boomer."

"Did you see that poor puppy running through the manor in terror? Of course she tried to hit him. Animals can sense that kind of thing."

Faith shrugged. "Boomer is a little bit timid."

Brooke was quiet.

Faith hoped her friend hadn't felt she was scolding her, but she wanted to be certain they knew the facts. Speculation wouldn't help solve Raymond's murder.

Or the mystery of the stolen scrimshaw.

The cat had traveled with his human to the manor dock twice. Along the way, he had detected the scents of predator animals and birds large enough to do damage to someone his size, despite his razor-sharp claws and needlelike teeth.

He needed muscle if he was going to visit the dock again. That muscle would be in the form of the extra-long black-and-brown dog.

The cat waited patiently by his friend's door. When a human pushed a cart into the room, the cat followed her inside. While she was busy cleaning the human version of a litter box, he quickly liberated the dog.

Rather than celebrating his freedom, the nervous dog cowered in a corner of his cage.

The cat strolled to the center of the room, sat, and groomed his left paw. Maybe if he gave the fellow some space, he would come to his senses and join him on an adventure.

Concerned he was running out of time, the cat turned to go. He was bowled over by the dog as he leaped from his confinement. The cat picked himself up, trying to regain some dignity.

The cat dashed to the doorway, paused, and waited.

His friend lowered himself even closer to the floor than he already was, his tail tucked between his stubby hind legs. Finally, he inched forward.

The cat patiently led the way downstairs. Soon they were outside in the brilliant sunshine scented with salt sea and the faintest hint of fish.

Hopefully large fish. Whale-size.

"Where are we going?" Brooke asked.

When they reached the top of the cliffs, Faith turned down the path toward the boathouse. "I'll show you the private dock."

"I have an idea," Brooke said as they walked. "For tomorrow night."

"Eileen doesn't want us to go to dinner with Milton."

"I know, but can we really pass up the opportunity to either eliminate or confirm him as a suspect?"

"How are we going to do that?" Faith asked.

"We'll have Milton meet us at my house," Brooke answered. "Diva and Bling will let me know whether Milton is a good or bad guy."

"I thought that only worked with a potential date," Faith said. She had her doubts about the ability of her friend's angelfish to detect men with dubious intentions. "You said this isn't a date."

"I won't tell Diva and Bling that. You are coming, aren't you? I might need backup."

"Well . . ." Faith didn't want her friend to face a potential killer alone. The angelfish wouldn't be able to defend Brooke from a maniac with a harpoon. "We have to let Eileen know."

"She already knows," Brooke said.

"You told her you're going?" Faith asked. "And she was okay with that?"

"Not exactly," Brooke said. "But she said we'd do what we wanted, remember? We can tell her after the fact. No need to make her worry, right?"

Faith felt torn. She was uncomfortable about deceiving her aunt. She slowed when the path descended more steeply, down steps carved into the hillside and paved with flat stones.

When the boathouse came into view, Brooke stopped and gasped. "It's so cute."

"Not that cute if someone used the boathouse as a staging area to commit a murder," Faith said. "They could have stolen the harpoon from the gallery, taken a motorboat to the north dock, killed Raymond, then returned without being seen."

"Why not put the harpoon back in the gallery?" Brooke asked.

"Maybe cleaning it would make it obvious it had been used." Faith felt queasy at the thought of a blood-covered harpoon. "Maybe the killer didn't have time."

A gust of briny-smelling wind ruffled the leafless branches surrounding the boathouse. Faith thought she caught a glimpse of black-and-white fur near the dock. This was getting ridiculous. She was imagining Watson everywhere. Maybe she needed to spend more time with her cat.

"It's too cold to eat here," Brooke said. "Let's go back to the garden, where we can be sheltered from the wind by the hedges."

Faith agreed and followed Brooke back up the path.

"So can I count on you tomorrow night?" Brooke asked.

"I'll be there." Faith couldn't let her friend go alone, whether Eileen approved or not. "What do I wear for a date with danger?"

The cat stopped abruptly. The dog plowed into him, knocking him flat on the wooden boards of the dock. He turned to swat the canine on the nose, but the poor fellow looked so contrite that he stopped his paw in midair.

When he heard voices, one belonging to his human, he darted behind a worn wooden box solidly affixed to the dock. The dog followed. The cat stood on his hind legs and peered over the box. His companion imitated him, rising to an amazing height.

When the humans turned and left, the cat trotted to the end of the dock. The salty breeze ruffled his fur. He sat down, watching the choppy waves for any sign of the large fish he had seen in the painting.

The dog huddled close to his side, but instead of watching the sea, his nose twitched, and he glanced nervously over his shoulder.

The cat could smell it too, although perhaps not as acutely as his canine friend.

The dog padded back toward the boathouse, snuffling at the air, the dock, and finally, the place where the boathouse met the gravel-covered ground.

The cat remained at the end of the dock until a gust of spray coated his fur with salty damp mist. He reluctantly gave up his vigil and joined his friend sniffing around the boathouse. The smell was very unpleasant. A large, white bird made a high-pitched peeping noise. Between the bird's squawking and the terrible odor, he felt his fur stand on end.

He'd had enough. The cat galloped to the path toward home.

The dog nearly ran him down in his haste to follow.

That evening, Watson curled up on Faith's lap in the cottage. He seemed unusually quiet for a cat who had been cooped up all day.

Faith was happy to have time to read and relax. It almost seemed too good to be true to have two uneventful evenings in a row.

But one thing disturbed Faith's peace of mind. Tomorrow evening she would help Brooke with her plan to either reveal a murderer or prove his innocence. Against her aunt's wishes.

Guilt pierced Faith's conscience. She hadn't exactly lied to Eileen, but she hadn't been honest with her either.

Faith had difficulty falling asleep, but once she finally did, she slept deeply until the alarm woke her.

Watson meowed when she didn't sit up immediately. He ate his breakfast so fast that Faith was afraid he would make himself sick. He swiped his pink tongue across his whiskers, then looked up at Faith as though demanding a second helping.

"I'm not giving you a double breakfast," Faith said. "Not when you've been lounging around the house all day."

Watson huffed his displeasure.

But she knew she'd made the right decision not to let her cat talk her into more food when he hopped onto the sofa and settled down to take a nap.

Faith was busy from the moment she unlocked the library doors until popular talks drew guests to the meeting rooms. She took advantage of the lull in activity to shelve books and straighten a stack of magazines on a table in a sitting area.

Marlene slipped into the library so quietly that Faith didn't hear her until the woman cleared her throat.

"Oh!" Faith nearly dropped the magazine she was holding.

"I didn't mean to startle you," Marlene said. Her wavy blonde hair was neatly styled, and her severe charcoal-gray suit and stylish heels were softened by a mauve silk blouse. She emanated her usual professional appearance, except for the way her gaze darted around the empty library.

Was the assistant manager on edge? Faith was not accustomed to seeing Marlene flustered. "Is there something I can help you with?" she asked.

Marlene's shoulders slumped, as though coming to Faith was the last thing she'd wanted to do. "I'm concerned about the rampant thievery. First the harpoon, then the *Essex* scrimshaw, and now the rest of Mrs. Prather's collection. It reflects poorly on the manor."

Faith could tell it took a lot for the woman to admit to any weakness.

"As much as I hate to see the manor's reputation sullied," Marlene continued, "I'm afraid it comes down to a lack of vigilance by the staff."

Faith wondered if Marlene was going to suggest she bore responsibility for the thefts. She felt herself bristling against the accusation, but she held her tongue. Marlene seemed to be in a talkative mood.

"I know you and your book club fancy yourselves amateur sleuths, trying to solve cases and whatnot. I wondered whether you had any ideas about the goings-on this week."

"I'll admit we've been keeping our eyes open," Faith said carefully. "But I wouldn't go so far as to say we're attempting to solve a case."

"Do you have any idea who might have stolen the items? If you know something, can you please tell me? My job may be on the line."

Faith wasn't about to share idle speculation with Marlene, and she highly doubted the Jaxons would fire her over something that was so clearly out of her control. But Marlene seemed rattled, and Faith wanted to reassure her. "The manor can't function without your guidance. I'm sure your judgment isn't in question. I don't know who the thief is, but your name never made it onto the suspect list."

Marlene shot Faith a smug smile. "I knew you were investigating." Then her smile faded. "Working at Castleton is a wonderful experience. I don't know what I'd do without my career here."

Marlene's tough facade seemed about to crack. Faith reached a hand to Marlene, but before she had the chance to offer any comfort or support, the woman spun on one heel and strode out of the library.

Faith was sure Marlene would never risk her position as assistant manager by doing anything morally questionable. Her career was her life. She had overcome difficult issues in her past to which she never wanted to return.

It most likely wasn't necessary, but Faith decided to put in a good word for Marlene with Wolfe. The library was empty, so she locked up and walked through the gallery. She hurried so as not to be tempted to eye the treasures on the vendor tables.

Wolfe's office was on the third floor, which was off-limits to guests and to most employees. Faith wasn't certain she would be welcome to barge in on his private quarters. She had nearly talked herself out of her mission to defend Marlene when she saw Wolfe in the lobby.

She waited until he finished a conversation with a guest, then headed toward him, her heels tapping across the marble floor. Faith didn't want to seem undignified by calling out his name as he climbed the stairs quickly. She followed, hoping to catch up, but his long-legged stride kept him well ahead of her.

Wolfe vanished up the final flight of steps before Faith could catch his attention.

Faith stood by the elevator on the second floor, debating how hard she wanted to press Marlene's defense. She turned to leave and saw Agnes coming down the hall.

Faith ducked behind a potted plant discreetly shading the elevator door, not entirely hidden but not out in the open either.

After reading about Agnes's bus accident, Faith knew why Agnes used a cane. When both her legs were broken, Agnes's Olympic dreams had been dashed. It was not Faith's place to judge, but she knew many people had suffered far worse and did not harbor the bitterness that seemed to color her attitude.

When Agnes reached the top of the stairs, she stumbled.

Faith's heart leaped to her throat as she feared the woman would tumble down the steps.

But Agnes grasped the stair railing, saving herself. She glared down at the object she had tripped over. A giraffe-shaped dog toy in a color that nearly matched the carpeting on the stairs. Agnes glanced around, then snatched up the chew toy. Pulling her arm back like a baseball pitcher, Agnes launched the toy down the stairs.

The toy landed on the floor of the lobby with a squeak.

Faith stifled a gasp at how far the toy had sailed. She couldn't imagine the frail-looking woman having that much upper-body strength. But perhaps gravity had done most of the work.

Agnes straightened with a triumphant gleam in her eyes. She grabbed the ornate handrail and walked down the stairs, struggling a bit.

What did I just see?

13

Faith was still staring at the stairs when the elevator doors dinged and opened.

Wolfe walked out and nearly bumped into Faith. He carried a thin laptop case and had a coat draped over his arm. "Oh, sorry. I didn't expect anyone to be right outside the doors."

"My fault." Faith gathered her scattered wits and adopted a professional tone. "I probably shouldn't bother you with this issue."

"You can talk to me anytime." Concern creased a line between his eyes. "Would you like to come to my office?" He glanced at his watch. "I'm headed to a meeting in Boston, but I can spare a few minutes."

"I don't want to keep you." Faith struggled not to look or sound foolish. "Marlene came to me this morning, concerned that she had somehow let the manor down."

Wolfe lifted one eyebrow. "How can she possibly think that? Marlene does a wonderful job. She's a bit strict sometimes, but she's extraordinarily organized and efficient. I don't know what we'd do without her."

"That's what I told her, but I got the impression she's afraid the recent thefts reflect poorly on her job performance. I think she's afraid she'll get fired."

"I do not hold her accountable for someone else's misconduct. She should know that by now."

"Marlene is really shaken," Faith said. "She may need a reminder from you."

"I'll talk to her when I get back this evening."

"It's probably best you don't mention I said anything," Faith added. "Marlene came to me in confidence, and she seemed reluctant to admit her fear."

Wolfe nodded. "Marlene is always putting up a brave front." He checked his watch again. "I apologize, but I really need to go. I'm certain the police will arrest the thief soon and everything will be resolved. Then we can all breathe easier."

Faith could only hope.

The cat congratulated himself for his impeccable timing as he followed a human into the room housing the Persian. Always the gentleman, he sat politely in the doorway.

The Persian's human was away at the moment, but the cat invited him in with an aloof tilt of her chin.

He strolled inside. If he hoped to escape unnoticed, he knew his time with her was limited. He jumped up onto the sofa next to the Persian's pillow.

She stood and stretched luxuriously, then hopped off the sofa.

He was a little startled to see her feet actually touch the floor, padded though it was with thick carpeting.

She made a small leap to the top of a coffee table, and he followed. A square device sat on the table. The Persian batted it delicately, causing a picture to appear. It was an image of her and her human. As always, the human held the Persian in her arms. They appeared to be on a ship, not unlike the one he had visited in Lighthouse Bay several days ago. Behind them was the sea. Leaping from the water was a whale.

Was the Persian merely showing a favored image of herself, or was she encouraging him? He gazed at her, drawn deep into blue eyes as beautiful as two fully stocked koi ponds.

The cat heard the rumble of the cart the human pushed. He touched his nose to the Persian's pert little pink nose, leaped off the table, and stealthily followed the cart out of the room.

He had to see one of the creatures for himself, even if it meant returning to the dock with the frightening smells.

When Faith returned to the cottage, Watson waited inside by the door. He didn't try to slip past her. Instead, he followed Faith to the kitchen in expectation of dinner.

She considered cutting back on his portions. He had lounged around the cottage all day. The cat didn't seem to be gaining weight, although his banishment from the manor might have been too soon to show up in added ounces packed onto his handsome body. She ended up feeding him full rations.

Faith changed into a skirt and a blouse, hoping she was dressed appropriately for dinner at The Captain's Table. The upscale restaurant was worthy of style, but Faith reminded herself that she was playing chaperone to Brooke in her crazy scheme, not going on a date.

She gave Watson a tunaroon, grabbed her coat, and left a little earlier than she needed to. When she arrived in town, she drove slowly by The Fishwife's Attic. She had more questions for Corrie about Raymond's purchase of a scrimshaw replica, but the *Closed* sign hung in the front window. Her questions would have to wait.

As soon as Faith rang the bell, Brooke opened the door and pulled her inside. "I'm almost ready. Just give me a few more minutes." She disappeared down the hall.

While Faith waited, she watched Diva and Bling as they drifted around their large tank, trailing long fins and tails like veils. Brooke decorated the tank in keeping with the elegant angelfish. Colorful glass pebbles were artfully arranged on a bed of sand. A faux diamond necklace had been draped over a ruby-red ceramic high heel. Live plants provided a touch of green, and a jewelry box opened regularly, emitting a stream of bubbles.

Precisely on time, the doorbell rang.

Brooke rushed into the room and joined Faith at the fish tank. "You greet Milton, and I'll keep an eye on Diva and Bling for their reaction."

When Faith opened the door, four people stood there: Milton in his suit and signature bow tie, Judith in a blue dress, Agnes in a gray wool pantsuit, and a dapper older gentleman with a neatly trimmed white goatee who was wearing a three-piece suit.

Faith heard violently splashing water behind her.

"Aha!" Brooke exclaimed. She turned to face the door, her eyes wide in surprise. "Oh. Hello."

"I hope you don't mind," Milton said. "I brought a few more guests. I've already notified the restaurant."

Faith tried to relax a little from the initial surprise. "The more the merrier," she said, immediately regretting her choice of words. How could a recent widow be merry?

"Good evening." The older man bowed slightly. "I'm attending the conference, but I don't believe I've made your acquaintance. I'm Rex Nelson, professor of literature and resident expert on Herman Melville's work." He smiled. "And no, I am not quite old enough to have met the great man in person."

Faith had a feeling it was going to be an entertaining evening. "I'm Faith Newberry, the Castleton Manor librarian and archivist."

"And we've met indirectly," Brooke said. "You sent your compliments to the kitchen for my clam chowder the other day. I'm Brooke Milner."

"Your culinary creations are unforgettable," Rex said. "And now your lovely face will likewise be indelibly imprinted upon my memory."

Faith thought he was laying it on a little thick, but Brooke seemed charmed.

"I would suggest we walk to the restaurant," Brooke said, "but I think it's too chilly tonight."

"We can all ride in my rental car," Rex offered.

"Brooke and I will go in my car," Faith said hastily. "I think that will be more convenient for everyone, since we'll be going home and you'll all be returning to the manor."

"Good thinking," Rex said.

Once they were in Faith's car, Brooke repeated Rex's statement. "Good thinking indeed. Now we can talk."

"I heard Diva and Bling splashing," Faith said.

"They almost jumped out of their tank. They must have imagined they were piranhas and planned to attack the killer."

"There's one big problem," Faith said. "To which one of the four were they reacting?"

Brooke sighed. "I can't believe my plan failed."

"Not completely." Faith wasn't entirely sold on the idea that Brooke's angelfish could detect a questionable human, but they had definitely reacted to something. "Maybe we can narrow it down to one of them."

The cat paced in front of the cottage's cold fireplace. What were the chances he could see a whale in the dark of night? Did the huge creatures go to sleep at night, like he did with his human in a comfy bed?

The image of the Persian and her human standing so close to a whale had driven him into a near frenzy. He could never capture one for his dinner. He knew when a potential meal outweighed his hunting abilities. Was catching just a glimpse of one too much to ask for?

When his human went out at night, she was typically gone for a long time. He could pace and stew about it, or he could take action.

Faith and Brooke made it to the restaurant first. By the time Milton, Rex, Judith, and Agnes arrived, their table was ready.

The hostess led them through the tastefully decorated dining room. Faith thought the hostess looked familiar. Maybe she had seen the elegant older woman in church or around Lighthouse Bay.

As they walked, Milton pulled Faith and Brooke aside. "I'm sure you're wondering why Judith and Agnes are joining us tonight. With the tragedy they're going through, I thought it would be nice for them to have an evening out. I hope you don't mind."

"Of course not," Brooke said.

"It was very considerate of you," Faith added. But she wondered why Milton neglected to explain why he had invited Rex.

The group sat down at a table covered with a crisp white tablecloth, and the hostess gave them menus.

"Dinner is my treat," Rex announced, waving a hand around the table. "Everyone, please order whatever strikes your fancy."

Brooke mulled over several exotic selections. She was obviously seeking new culinary inspiration.

Faith decided on a simpler dish that would not distract her from questioning suspects. A little dread chilled her spine when she considered that one of the people sitting at the table could be a killer. If only the angelfish could tell them which one.

Then another chill of dread crept up her spine. She nudged Brooke and nodded toward the door. Wolfe was helping his mother out of her cashmere coat.

"Oh no," Brooke whispered. "I hope they're not upset that we're having dinner with the guests."

Faith briefly considered covering her face with the menu, but that would never work. She was glad she had already made her selection, because her brain had turned to mush.

"Our Castleton Manor hosts," Rex declared. "What a happy coincidence."

Not happy, Faith thought. One glance at Brooke's pale face told her that she felt the same. They were helpless to interfere as Rex waved at Wolfe and Charlotte.

Wolfe glanced at Faith and Brooke, huddled together like two naughty schoolgirls who were about to be sent to the principal's office. Was he angry, or was that amusement crinkling the corners of his blue eyes?

"Mr. Jaxon," Rex said, "won't you and your beautiful date join us?"

"Mother, what do you think?" Wolfe asked Charlotte. "Should we have a quiet dinner by ourselves, or should we join this group?"

"I think I would quite enjoy myself with these fine people."

Faith wasn't certain whether she had imagined it, but she thought Charlotte winked at her. What must the proper manor owner and literary event hostess think of employees dining with guests? Faith wished she had listened to Eileen.

"I certainly feel as though I'm having dinner at the captain's table now," Milton said as the waitstaff rearranged the table to accommodate two more diners.

"Better yet, we are at the captain's table at The Captain's Table," Rex said with a hearty laugh. He was obviously a man who enjoyed life.

They ordered their meals and were soon enjoying delicious salads with a variety of ingredients and presentations that Faith found stunning. Milton clearly enjoyed a Caesar salad with fresh croutons and thick shavings of Parmesan cheese. Brooke gushed over a grilled shrimp salad, praising every element of it. Faith tucked into her salad of mild goat cheese, delicate greens, and bits of candied pecan. It was more like a dessert than a salad, and she ate every bite.

Rex turned his attention from his arugula-and-beet salad to

Charlotte. "You must wonder how a mature gentleman like myself landed a date with four lovely young women."

Faith thought it was nice of him to include Judith and Agnes. The sisters glowed with delight.

"But this is not actually a date," Rex continued.

"No?" Wolfe asked, smiling.

Rex turned to Brooke. "I have to confess my subterfuge. I asked Milton if I could tag along so I could beg for your clam chowder recipe."

"And I invited Miss Milner to dinner to thank her for saving Captain Boomer from a fall down the front steps," Milton said. "Dachshunds have delicate backs, and he could have hurt himself quite badly if not for her."

Faith snuck a glance at Wolfe and Charlotte. She hoped they would forgive her and Brooke for going out with guests. Judging from their amused expressions, though, they didn't seem to mind.

By the time their entrées arrived, everyone seemed to be having a grand time, including Judith. Faith felt relieved that the woman was able to enjoy an evening of relief from her anguish. Wolfe answered questions about the construction of the replica whaling ship, and Charlotte talked about the history of Castleton Manor.

Faith sliced into her red snapper. It would have been nice to focus solely on her delicious meal and the company of her handsome boss and his mother. Instead, she studied Milton, Rex, Judith, and Agnes, wondering which one of them had caused Diva and Bling to nearly jump out of their tank in an apparent attempt to protect Brooke.

Which one of them had the capacity for murder?

14

By dessert, Rex was deep in discussion of his area of expertise—the novel *Moby-Dick*. While Milton complained that the sections spent describing whales slowed the action, Rex argued that they increased the reader's appreciation for the hunting scenes.

"I have to admit I found some passages of the novel tedious," Wolfe said.

Rex shook his head vigorously. "By presenting the anatomy and habits of whales, Melville raises the tension. You are acutely aware of how dangerous the animals can be—"

Milton waved his dessertspoon, interrupting Rex. "On the contrary, while reading *Moby-Dick* for the first time as a young college student, I fervently wished for a harpoon through my heart to end my misery." His face flushed as red as a cooked lobster as he realized his error.

The diners sat in stunned silence for a moment.

"Mr. Waldrin," Charlotte said softly, "your enthusiasm may prove disturbing to some of your tablemates." She nodded slightly toward Judith, who was concentrating on her dessert dish, and Agnes sitting beside her.

Judith glanced up, obviously realizing everyone was looking at her. "This dessert is exquisite," she said.

Agnes nodded. "It's the best I've had during my entire stay in Lighthouse Bay."

Faith relaxed a little. The women had missed the entire exchange.

"I am so sorry, Mrs. Prather and Ms. VanStuth," Milton said.

"You aren't responsible for the quality of the food at the manor," Agnes replied.

Milton appeared startled, and he raised his eyebrows slightly. Beside her, Brooke stiffened. Faith thought concern flickered in Charlotte's eyes, and Wolfe opened his mouth to say something.

"We gentlemen have erred in our choice of dinner conversation if we have lost the attention of our gracious companions," Rex broke in before Wolfe could speak.

Charlotte cast a benevolent smile at him.

"Wise words, Mr. Nelson," Wolfe said. "I would be devastated if the ladies decided to escape our discussion by leaving before we finish our coffee and dessert."

Had Faith imagined that Wolfe watched her when he said those words? She could feel heat rise to her cheeks as she glanced down, pretending the cloth napkin on her lap needed adjusting. Sometimes Wolfe was so friendly and kind that a woman could forget he was her boss and leap to wild conclusions. It wasn't as if the dinner had been planned.

Faith decided to do her part to steer the conversation to safer topics. She turned to Judith and Agnes. "I'm happy you both could join us this evening."

"Why wouldn't we?" Agnes asked tartly. "We needed a break from the same old tired conference food."

"Oh dear," Charlotte said. "I wish you had informed Wolfe or me that something wasn't to your liking. Would you mind if we discussed it in private soon?"

"I doubt it'll help," Agnes grumbled.

Didn't Agnes realize Brooke was the head chef for Castleton Manor and responsible for that so-called tired food? Faith glanced at Brooke and noticed two fierce dots of red coloring her cheeks. Faith couldn't tell whether her friend was embarrassed or angry.

Faith scrambled to think of something to say to change the subject. "I thought you might be attending your nephew's birthday party tonight, Mrs. Prather."

"What nephew?"

Great. Now Judith was going to make Faith look like a fool in front of her boss. That would be two strikes against her. First, fraternizing with guests, and second, antagonizing them with ridiculous questions.

Faith couldn't even defend herself by stating she had heard from Corrie Baker that Raymond had purchased a scrimshaw replica for their nephew's birthday. That would reveal she had been snooping for clues. Not a good thing to admit in front of potential killers.

"I must be mistaken," Faith said. "Perhaps that was another guest who spoke about a nephew."

"Apparently so. Neither my late husband nor I have a nephew," Judith said, then returned her attention to her dessert.

Maybe Corrie had gotten the story wrong. Or maybe Raymond had made up a tale about a nephew.

But why would he purchase a replica for himself? And where was the *Essex* scrimshaw?

A gust of wind swept salty spray from the sea onto the dock. The cat winced and shrank back. The whales must have been sensibly bedded down for the evening. Their mission had been a bust. He turned and jogged up the dock to the boathouse.

The dog followed, looking miserable. His short fur offered little protection from the weather.

As they neared the boathouse, the dog stopped and sniffed.

The cat caught a faint odor. Not fish. That same something bad they'd both smelled earlier. He crouched low to the ground and inched forward one paw at a time. He stepped on a wet spot, lifted his paw and gave it a shake, then continued. He glanced behind to check on his friend.

The dog was already low to the ground, but he managed to go a notch lower as he followed.

They reached the back of the boathouse. The cat wiggled his nose, trying to zero in on the scent. Mist dampened the fresh gravel. A combination of earthy dust and briny water confused his smelling ability.

The canine seemed undeterred, his nose wrinkling as he determined the nature and direction of the bad odor.

He had to admit that dogs might have the advantage over cats in the olfactory area.

The dog shied away from the base of the shed and trotted toward the walking path, but the cat leaped in front of him, blocking his way. The cat strolled back to the shed and pawed at the base of the building. He lacked the paw power to remove gravel, but that was what his friend was born for, with his sturdy, powerful claws.

At first, the dog pretended not to understand.

The cat refused to budge, even though his fur was damp and crusty with salt. There was nothing he wanted more than to return to his warm home. Cleaning his handsome black-and-white fur was going to be an unpleasant chore.

The cat pawed at the gravel, then stared at his companion.

The dog huffed out a sigh, glanced nervously around the boat dock, and plowed into the gravel under the boathouse. He pitched gravel between his two hind legs with machinelike rhythm.

After finishing dessert, the group got up from the table, and Wolfe, Milton, and Rex assisted the ladies with their wraps.

As Wolfe helped Faith into her coat, he whispered, "Whatever you're up to, please be careful."

"Wolfe," Charlotte said, "we should give Faith a ride home."

"Thank you for the offer," Faith said, "but I drove to town."

"Then we'll follow you back to the manor," Wolfe said.

Brooke jumped in. "Actually, Faith and I need to discuss the themed hors d'oeuvre trays for her talk Thursday, so we're going back to my place first."

"But thank you again," Faith added.

Wolfe nodded, and they said goodbye.

Once inside her car, Faith was able to relax. She turned to Brooke in the passenger seat. "That was fast thinking."

"I really did think about the snacks," Brooke admitted. "You're going to compare novels like *Moby-Dick* with works by Louisa May Alcott and Jane Austen. Maybe I could prepare one tray of delicate tea cakes and finger sandwiches and another of dried cod and hardtack."

Faith laughed. "Let me guess which one would be consumed." She pulled out of the lot and headed to Brooke's apartment.

"All right, let's discuss the dinner. It sounds like Agnes hates the food at the manor." Brooke clenched her fists. "Ooh, she made me mad!"

"Did Agnes even realize you're the chef?" Faith asked. "Her comments insulted Charlotte and Wolfe too."

"Speaking of Wolfe," Brooke began, a gleam in her blue eyes, "what did he whisper to you as we left?"

"Nothing romantic, if that's what you're imagining," Faith said. "He told me to be careful. He could tell we weren't there to fraternize with the guests."

"Thank goodness for that. You wouldn't want Wolfe to think you weren't available because you were dating Milton or Rex."

"Both of them are perfectly nice gentlemen."

"I'm kind of glad Judith and Agnes came along. That way, Wolfe couldn't imagine we were double-dating."

"Okay, enough about Wolfe. Which guest did Diva and Bling react to?"

"I still don't know," Brooke said. "It occurs to me that they might not even have been reacting to a murderer. Maybe one of them is a garden-variety deadbeat or some other type of loser."

Once the dog got started, the cat was afraid he would dig a tunnel all the way to town. Gravel and dirt flew out of the hole with frightening speed.

Suddenly, the digging stopped.

The cat peered cautiously into the dark hole, fearing a face full of dirt. Instead, he saw his friend's hind end.

The dog was waddling backward, struggling to drag out a long, cloth-covered object.

Eager to help, the cat squeezed into the hole, mindful that his fur was receiving a coating of damp earth. Well, it couldn't be avoided.

Together they pulled the long, heavy cloth onto the coarse grass behind the boathouse. The cat patted the cloth, then sunk his claws into it and tugged. It was fastened with a rope. They both bit and tore at the wrapping.

A fold opened, and the canine pounced on a small cream-colored object.

The item resembled a lump of congealed cream, but the cat knew it wasn't food. There was one like it on his human's table in the cottage. He had licked it once, just to be sure, and it did not taste like cream one little bit.

His companion began to bite the object like a favorite chew toy, so the cat patted a paw on his nose to stop him. That was no chew toy.

He wasn't certain why it was important, but he had heard his human talking about the lumps as though they were as valuable as tunaroons.

A light from the cottage up the hill flashed on.

The dog lifted the object delicately in his mouth. Then cat and dog raced up the walking path toward the manor.

Faith parked in front of the cottage. The stone walls looked cold in the November night, but when she opened the front door, light and warmth flooded the stoop.

"I'm home," she called. "Watson?"

He wasn't on the sofa or the chair near the fireplace. Faith flicked on the kitchen light. No Watson.

"I have got to find out how he's escaping," she muttered to herself. "And then put an end to his wandering at will."

She had heard that cats used their whiskers to determine whether they could squeeze through spaces, but she was pretty sure Watson slipped into spaces much narrower than the span of his white whiskers.

Faith shed her coat and set her purse down. She was ready to unwind for a few minutes before going to bed. Thursday morning, she would present her talk contrasting men's adventure novels with women's fiction in the 1800s. She needed a good night's rest, but she could not sleep knowing Watson was roaming around at night.

She changed shoes, remembering his last excursion to the private boat dock beyond the cliffs. Then she put on a heavy coat. Ready to face the cold night, Faith opened the front door.

Watson meowed.

Faith dropped her keys. "You startled me."

She retrieved the keys, then held the door as Watson strolled into the cottage. She almost didn't recognize her cat. The white sections of his fur coat were as dark as the black.

"Hold on just a moment," Faith said. "Your paws are muddy. You're not walking on the carpet."

She reached for him, but Watson bounded away into the kitchen. At least he hadn't jumped on the furniture.

Muddy paw prints trailed across the floor. She followed them to their source. Watson sat beside his food bowl, waiting for his treat.

"I only give rewards when I come home and you've been good."

Faith waved a hand around. "I have no idea where you've been, and now you've made a mess of the floors."

Watson did not appear to feel the least bit guilty. He looked at his empty bowl, then up at Faith.

"No treat until I get you cleaned up."

Faith ran warm water in the kitchen sink and added a capful of pet shampoo. She set towels on the counter. Then she picked up Watson. He squirmed in her hands, slick with mud, but he didn't escape. She plopped him into the sink.

Faith had heard stories about cats and baths that resulted in humans with shredded shirtsleeves, even blood drawn. She had given Watson baths since he was a kitten so he would be accustomed to the process, but it had been a while since he'd received a full-blown sink bath.

A low, disgruntled growl rumbled in Watson's chest, but he behaved.

"Well, I'm sorry, but you need it. There's that handsome face," Faith said, carefully dabbing a washcloth around Watson's whiskers. "I wish you could talk. I would love to know how you got to be such a mess."

After Faith had thoroughly rinsed the frothy suds out of Watson's fur, she patted him with towels. When the majority of the water was gone, she set the blow-dryer to low and aimed it at him. Watson did not seem to mind this part. He stood still while Faith smoothed a brush over his fur, alternating with gentle gusts from the blow-dryer.

Faith wrapped Watson in a fresh towel and carried him to the living room. "I'll clean the floor tomorrow." She yawned. "I was going to review my notes for my talk, but you took up all my time."

Watson wiggled out of the towel. He stood on the arm of the chair, reached out with one paw, and batted a piece of decorative scrimshaw off the end table and onto the floor.

Now that she had seen the real thing, Faith was convinced the scrimshaw that had come with her cottage was merely a tourist-quality replica, meant to augment the New England decor. She didn't mind.

She would have been uncomfortable with the real thing now that she knew how valuable it was.

Watson started to hop down to chase after the scrimshaw, but Faith grabbed him.

"All warm and dry?" she asked. "I'm ready for bed."

Watson meowed. He had behaved during his bath, and now he obviously expected a reward.

"I guess you can have a tunaroon before we turn in." She detoured into the kitchen and placed a treat in his dish.

Watson gobbled it down, then looked to Faith for more.

"Your appetite has been huge this week. Now I know you haven't been staying home like you're supposed to. You've been escaping and running around. You're burning extra calories." Faith gave Watson a small portion of dry kibble instead of another tunaroon, which seemed to placate him.

Soon they were snuggled in bed. But Faith couldn't sleep. She thought of Eileen's warning not to go through with Brooke's plan to capture a killer at dinner.

Everything had turned out fine, but still, Faith knew she had to confess to her aunt. It wouldn't be easy, but honesty was the best policy.

She glanced at the time. Eileen struggled with rheumatoid arthritis, and sometimes she had difficulty sleeping. Faith didn't dare call her at this hour and risk disturbing her if she was having a good night's rest. She resolved to call first thing in the morning. Eileen would be up early, preparing for her workday at the library.

Once she made up her mind to talk to Eileen, sleep came easily.

Her rest was haunted by dreams of whales with designs etched into their teeth, as well as a feeling in the back of her mind that she was missing something.

15

"Could you meet me at Snickerdoodles for a quick cup of coffee?" Faith asked. She had finished getting herself and Watson ready for the day, then promptly called her aunt.

"I was hoping you'd call," Eileen said. "I can be there in fifteen minutes. What is it that's so urgent?"

"I'll tell you when I see you."

When Faith walked into Snickerdoodles, it was packed with morning commuters. She had second thoughts about confessing her escapade with Brooke where people might overhear. Lighthouse Bay was a small town, and news traveled fast.

Eileen sat at a table in the corner. She paused in her knitting to wave at Faith. Her aunt had dressed for the cool autumn weather in a soft green tweed skirt with a matching collarless jacket.

After Faith got a cup of coffee and a pastry from the counter, she sat across the table from her aunt.

Eileen rubbed her wrists and hands. Her arthritis must have been acting up in the cool, damp weather. "I'm ready to hear all about your evening." She smiled and leaned back in her chair as though awaiting the telling of a grand tale.

How had she known Faith and Brooke went through with their plan against her advice?

"That's why I wanted to meet you this morning," Faith said. "To tell you about dinner. But it sounds like you already know what happened. Did Brooke call you?"

Eileen shook her head. "I have other sources. A little birdie saw you at The Captain's Table in the company of a certain handsome Castleton Manor gentleman. I learned this bit of news when I stopped to mail a letter at the post office earlier this morning."

Faith wondered if Eileen's information source was the restaurant hostess she'd thought she recognized. Lighthouse Bay was indeed a small town.

"I want to hear everything about your date with Wolfe," Eileen continued.

"It wasn't a date," Faith said. "Brooke and I went to dinner with Milton Waldrin, Judith Prather, Agnes VanStuth, and another gentleman from the conference named Rex Nelson. We ran into Wolfe and Charlotte quite by accident."

Eileen raised one eyebrow in an expression of mild disapproval.

"I'm sorry I didn't listen to you. I know everything could have gone wrong, from getting reprimanded by my boss for fraternizing with guests to having an encounter with a murderer."

"You may still have had that encounter, but at least you were in the company of a crowd." Eileen began knitting again. "So you weren't on a date. You and Brooke were sleuthing. Fill me in on what happened."

Faith told her about the evening and concluded with an observation. "Judith seemed to appreciate a break from her grief, but Agnes was so rude. She might be an exceptionally unemotional person about the death of her brother-in-law, but Brooke thought it was odd too."

"Perhaps the reality of the situation hasn't hit her yet," Eileen suggested. "She may still be in denial."

"I know I should give Agnes the grace to mourn in her own way, even if it seems strange to me. This isn't the first blow she's received after all."

"Few of us come through this life unscathed," Eileen remarked.

Faith knew that was true. She had a dream job now and good friends in a quaint little town. But before that, she had suffered heartbreak that had left her hesitant to open herself to the possibility of love again.

"Agnes may look frail now, but she was an Olympic hopeful in her youth." Faith described how the bus crash had ended Agnes's athletic dreams, leaving her using a cane.

Eileen folded her knitting and put it away. "What sport was she pursuing?"

"The article said she was on a track-and-field team, but it didn't mention her specialty."

"I have more questions," Eileen said, "but I need to open the library."

"I need to open a library too," Faith replied. "I'm sorry I didn't tell you about going to dinner with Brooke beforehand."

"I appreciate that you told me now," Eileen said. "Just remember, in Lighthouse Bay, people can rarely hide their secrets."

Faith felt a burden had been lifted off her shoulders. Thank goodness she had decided to confess. As an added bonus, her aunt could also squelch any crazy rumors floating around town about Faith going on a date with Wolfe.

The gallery was buzzing with conversation as Faith walked through on her way to the library. She slowed to gaze at the ivory hair comb in the display case. *Still there.*

The friendly vendor moved close, her voice low. "Did you hear?"

That was a rather nonspecific question, so Faith shook her head.

"The police found the murder weapon," the woman said. "A harpoon. *The* harpoon." She waved a hand at the museum display where the antique harpoon had been.

Faith's stomach clenched at the memory of the harpoon sailing across the dock. "Where?" Her voice was a hoarse whisper.

The vendor shrugged. "I don't know."

The guests and vendors in the gallery were likely to offer only wild speculation. Faith resisted the urge to gather more of what was undoubtedly baseless information. Instead, she focused on reaching the library.

As soon as she opened the door, a couple claimed velvet-cushioned chairs in front of the fireplace. After a brief exchange of morning greetings, they ignored Faith. The man read a history book while the woman leafed through a Boston newspaper. Another guest entered and began poring over the map collection.

Faith took the opportunity to study her notes for her midmorning talk.

Before she got far, Midge stepped into the library. Her friend carried her black medical bag. Her shoulder-length blonde hair was pulled back, and her fingernails were painted pink with one tiny purple paw print on each nail.

Midge approached Faith's desk, glanced around, then leaned close. "Can you talk?" She motioned to a far corner of the room.

Was everyone in a conspiratorial mood today? Faith nodded, then followed. "What's going on?"

"I was asked to make a house call this morning to check on Mr. Waldrin's dachshund."

"Is he okay?" Faith asked.

"I couldn't find anything wrong with him," Midge answered.

"So what happened?"

"Mr. Waldrin woke to find Boomer coated with mud. The problem is, Boomer stays in a kennel at night. The poor man was completely baffled. Clean dog goes in the kennel before dinner last night, and a muddy dog emerges this morning. All I could do was suggest Mr. Waldrin take Boomer to the pet spa to have him cleaned up."

The manor offered both a human and a pet spa. Guests could be pampered, and so could their pets.

"That is strange," Faith said. "Why didn't Milton notice Boomer was muddy until this morning?"

"Mr. Waldrin claimed Boomer was sound asleep when he got back from dinner," Midge said. "The poor puppy doesn't sleep well away from home, so Milton didn't want to wake him."

"He's certain Boomer was already muddy?" Faith asked. "He couldn't have gotten out while Milton was asleep?"

Midge shook her head. "Mr. Waldrin told me he's a light sleeper and that's why Boomer stays in a kennel at night."

That confirmed what Faith suspected. She leaned closer to Midge and whispered, "I haven't mentioned this to anyone, but Watson came home last night caked with mud. He didn't get the spa treatment, but I did give him a bath in the kitchen sink. And this morning, I learned that the murder weapon was found."

"Do you think—" Midge began. "No, it has to be a coincidence that Watson and Boomer were both muddy. Someone must have released Boomer from his kennel. Milton insists it was latched."

"Milton was at dinner with me and Brooke last night, so it couldn't have been him," Faith said. "But I don't know who else would have done it."

Midge's green eyes flashed with annoyance, probably at being left out of the adventure. "I thought Eileen had talked you two out of going."

Faith winced at the memory of their deception. "We failed to mention to her that we decided to go through with Brooke's plan." She told Midge about how Diva and Bling had reacted when the guests arrived and their inability to determine to whom the angelfish had responded. She briefly described the dinner—running into Wolfe and his mother, as well as Agnes's rude behavior. "I confessed to Eileen this morning, so now everyone in our book group knows all the details."

"You have been very busy," Midge said. "So who let Boomer out? And where did he go?"

"Watson has discovered some way to escape the cottage. He and Boomer seem to be buddies. Maybe someone released Boomer and Watson followed. What if the killer took Boomer along to hide the murder weapon? If only that cat could talk."

"You're assuming Mr. Waldrin is innocent. If there's one thing we've learned unraveling mysteries, it's never make assumptions, especially when it comes to murder. He could have gone out after dinner with you. He picked up Boomer and took him someplace muddy to bury the weapon. And Watson followed."

"But Watson showed up right after I got home. The timing doesn't work for Milton to be involved."

"Maybe he did all of it before dinner," Midge suggested.

There were still some pieces missing, but Faith had to admit that Midge's theory made sense. And Midge was right that Faith needed to be careful not to let her opinion of the seemingly mild-mannered Mr. Waldrin and his adorable dachshund cloud her judgment.

"We don't have enough information yet to figure it out," Faith said finally.

"You need more data, Sherlock?" Midge teased. "Hey, I need to get back to my clinic."

Soon after Midge left, it was time for Faith to give her lecture. She was pleased that the rows of cushioned chairs in the salon were nearly all occupied. That made the time she had spent developing an entertaining presentation worthwhile.

The audience seemed interested to learn that the rousing adventure novel *Moby-Dick*, published in 1851, did not sell well in the author's lifetime. It didn't achieve acclaim as a classic in American literature until years later.

In contrast, *Little Women*, written by Louisa May Alcott and published in the late 1860s, was an immediate commercial success. The novel's inclusion in the canon of classic American literature came as women's fiction gained academic approval.

Whatever their journeys, both novels had stood the test of time.

Clearly her audience agreed. The crowd stayed rapt and engaged throughout her talk.

The cat strolled into the pet spa and watched his friend from a discreet corner, his whiskers twitching in a smirk. If only the humans knew he had been in nearly as disreputable a state as the dog.

But the canine seemed content to be washed, trimmed, dried, and massaged by the capable hands of the pet spa staff.

The cat was glad that his cleanup had been at the hands of his human in the privacy of the cottage. Being bathed was enough of an indignity without it being performed by strangers.

The dog's human arrived, making pleased sounds at his pet's tidy appearance. The spa humans had even cleaned and pressed the dog's bow tie.

All seemed well with the world until the human in the uniform arrived. The cat had met him many times, as his human often stuck her nose where it did not belong—a trait she had no doubt picked up from her inquisitive cat. He could sense the alarm exuding from every human in the spa, although the uniformed man only seemed interested in the dog's human.

The man with the bow tie that matched his dog's smelled of fear as he spoke to the uniformed man. Finally, the human lowered his head sadly. He left the pet spa with the uniformed man following him.

The spa humans made an even greater fuss over the dog when he made stressed snuffling noises. Once he calmed down, they gave him a treat and put him in a cage.

The cat hopped down from his perch and walked over to his friend. He had heard his human talk about the uniformed humans locking bad humans in cages.

Maybe that was what had happened to the dog's person. He couldn't imagine how a human could fit inside one of the little cages. He hoped they came in different sizes.

16

As Faith left the salon after finishing her talk, she heard a new commotion coming from the gallery. People crowded around the French doors, faces pressed to the cold glass, watching as the police escorted Milton to a Lighthouse Bay police cruiser. He wasn't wearing handcuffs. Faith hoped that meant he wasn't being arrested.

The police fetching Milton from the manor might be the additional information Faith told Midge they needed. And yet she found no satisfaction in thinking this could be the solution to the murder. Not if it involved Milton and his dachshund in their sweet matching bow ties.

"Boomer!" Faith exclaimed out loud. The shy dog must be terrified. She jogged to the front desk in the lobby. "Excuse me."

Cara, the clerk on duty, glanced up from the registration desk's computer screen. "Yes? How may I help you?"

"I should probably ask Marlene, but this is kind of an emergency. Would it be possible to check Mr. Waldrin's room?"

The young woman appeared uncomfortable. "You're right. That would be a decision for Ms. Russell. Why do you need to check his room? Housekeeping was just making their rounds."

"I'm worried that his dachshund might have been left alone in the room." And might be there for a long time, depending on what the police decided about Milton's guilt or innocence.

Cara smiled. "Mr. Waldrin took Boomer to the pet spa early this morning. The dog was covered with mud. I remember clearly because Mr. Waldrin asked me for directions to the spa. The poor thing was bundled up in a blanket. I'm sure the dog is still there."

Marlene swept up to the front desk at that moment, all confidence and authority.

Faith was relieved to see that the assistant manager had regained her composure.

"Is everything okay?" Marlene asked.

"Not exactly," Faith said. She gave Marlene the news about Milton leaving the manor in a police cruiser. "I was checking on his dog, but Cara told me Mr. Waldrin took Boomer to the pet spa this morning."

"People and their pets." Marlene wrinkled her nose as if she smelled something offensive.

While Charlotte insisted Castleton Manor literary events be pet friendly, Marlene made her distaste for animals and their doting humans known. To the staff, anyway. Faith doubted a guest had ever realized how Marlene really felt about their precious animal companions. Marlene might be difficult at times, but she was the consummate professional.

"I'll check to make sure the spa staff know what's going on," Faith said.

Marlene was more than happy to leave the care of a guest's pet to the librarian.

"Don't forget you are expected at the buffet lunch today," Marlene told her. "The guests like to have access to the day's lecturers and workshop presenters in case they have additional questions."

"I'll be there," Faith promised.

She dropped by the pet spa and gave the staff her cell phone number. If Milton didn't arrive to pick up Boomer by closing time, Faith volunteered to take the dachshund. As nice as Castleton's kennels were, she couldn't imagine that the timid dog would be comfortable there.

When her cell phone pinged, Faith excused herself to check the message.

It was a text from Brooke. *Murder weapon found.*

Faith replied, *A vendor told me this morning, but she didn't know where.*

Under the boathouse, Brooke texted. *Just overheard the police telling Wolfe.*

After they finished comparing notes, Faith headed for the library. She paused by the statue of Agatha Christie.

"Any suggestions?" she asked the mystery author. Of course, she didn't expect an answer, but perhaps she could gain inspiration in her pursuit of the solution to Raymond's murder. She was even more motivated now that Milton had been taken in for questioning.

Walking through the gallery, she slowed by Owen's table. The scrimshander wore a jewelry loupe connected to one lens of his eyeglasses. He worked on a piece, carving delicate lines with a special knife. He certainly took his art seriously.

As Faith watched, she reviewed what she had learned.

Corrie from The Fishwife's Attic said Raymond had purchased a scrimshaw replica from her to give to his nephew for his birthday. Yet according to Judith, neither she nor Raymond had a nephew.

Judith claimed Raymond had met a scrimshander on the dock. Tasi suggested Raymond might have been buying a piece with questionable provenance. He might have even illegally acquired scrimshaw.

Tasi and Milton had an obvious reason to be angry with Raymond. The man had called their knowledge into question, insulting them publicly. Both of them had the motive and opportunity to throw a harpoon into Raymond's heart.

Had Raymond insulted Owen too? Faith hadn't looked into the scrimshander's whereabouts that night.

Owen was ignoring Faith.

"Hello," she said.

He grunted an unintelligible response. The man simply refused to converse with her.

Faith was convinced he knew something. He definitely appeared strong enough to throw a harpoon.

She glanced toward the library and noticed three people waiting patiently. Owen the scrimshander would be in the gallery for the rest of the week. Faith could question him another time. The police were obviously on the job. Even if she was certain they had taken the wrong man to the station.

Now she had to get to work. She hurried to the library and unlocked the door.

At the luncheon buffet, Faith took a seat at Tasi's table.

Tasi looked like an island princess, her black hair in a braid that circled her head like a crown. She wore a long dress in a bright tropical print. A shawl was draped over her shoulders as a concession to the November chill, although the manor was warmly heated. The beautiful Persian cat, Alika, seemed happy to perch in her owner's lap, accepting nibbles of food.

Many guests wanted to sit with the charismatic woman, including Rex. He dressed in a more casual style than he had for dinner at The Captain's Table. Today he wore a cardigan over a dress shirt and a tie.

The other guests at the table asked Tasi questions about Hawaiian history and culture. Some quizzed her about possible vacation destinations as well.

Faith had questions of her own, but she waited until the lunch conversation dwindled to discussions of the local weather. Then she turned to Tasi and said, "I learned that some modern scrimshaw is modeled after historical pieces."

"That is true," Tasi answered.

"That hardly seems fair." Rex frowned. "Copying someone else's art?"

"Imitation is the sincerest form of flattery," another guest said.

"What if I want to buy the real thing but purchase a copy by mistake?" Rex asked.

Faith followed the conversation intently. She couldn't have gotten answers better if she'd written a script.

"An expert in the art can tell the difference between authentically historical scrimshaw art and modern replicas," Tasi replied.

"How?" one of the other guests asked.

"Scrimshaw is a living art. I have an example." Tasi reached inside her tote bag and extracted two pieces. One had been loose in the bag, and the other was inside a padded jewelry box. She handed both to Rex. "Tell me what you see. But don't touch the one in the case. The oils from your hands can stain ivory because it's porous."

Rex's brow creased as he studied the scrimshaw, then passed it to the woman on his right.

The scrimshaw pieces made it around the table, with murmured comments by the diners.

Faith noticed the one in the jewelry case had a patina of age that made the ivory a rich deep color, and the carving of a whale was smoothed on the edges. The other piece was a bright white, and the carved whale seemed to have crisp edges.

"Do you see the difference?" Tasi asked.

"It's quite obvious," Rex said. "However, a person might deliberately age a piece and pass it off as historical. It happens all the time with antiques. Some stores sell distressed furniture deliberately designed to look much older than it is."

Tasi nodded. "And some replicas can be quite good."

"What if the *Essex* scrimshaw was a fake?" Faith blurted. "A really good replica?"

"That would be unfortunate," Rex said. "As I understand it, Mrs. Prather spent an enormous sum for that piece."

"Now that it's gone, there is no way to authenticate it," Tasi said.

"My husband is an insurance adjuster," the woman seated next to Rex said. "Without authentication, Mrs. Prather's insurance company may refuse to cover its loss."

Tasi rubbed her cat's head with one hand, then shrugged. "If only the Prathers had allowed Mr. Waldrin and me to examine the scrimshaw when we asked, we could have assisted with the insurance claim."

The gesture and the words seemed casual, but Faith detected an undercurrent of anger in the woman.

It did seem odd that Raymond had been opposed to letting anyone see the *Essex* scrimshaw. If he doubted the skills claimed by Tasi or Milton, there were other experts in the manor this week. There had been no need to wait until after the conference to have it appraised in Boston.

An idea formed in Faith's mind. There was an expert right here in the manor. Owen the scrimshander.

If she could just get him to talk.

After lunch, Faith made a side trip to her cottage. With all the stress of the last few days, plus giving her presentation that morning, she wanted nothing more than to unwind for a few minutes before returning to the library.

The conference ended tomorrow evening. All the guests—and suspects—would leave the manor. Faith didn't have much time to solve the mystery of Raymond's murder.

She unlocked the front door and opened it a crack, anticipating an escape attempt by Watson. But the cottage was empty.

"That little rascal," Faith said to herself. "I've got to find out how he's escaping."

Faith picked up the scrimshaw Watson had knocked to the floor last night. The piece, decorated with a leaping dolphin, had come with the cottage, along with a few nice pieces of antique furniture.

She was certain the scrimshaw was a replica. The Jaxons kept their valuable scrimshaw collection on the third floor in their private living quarters when it wasn't on display under lock and key in the library. She pocketed it. Maybe she could use it as a conversation starter to do some subtle investigating later.

Faith glanced around the cozy living room, longing for a cup of tea served with no drama. She sighed, then put on her coat and scarf and headed back to the manor.

She had barely settled in when Laura entered the library dressed in her housekeeper's uniform. The young woman's pale face was splotchy, and Faith worried that something awful had happened to her.

"Can I talk to you?" Laura whispered.

"Let's step over here." Faith led the way to the quiet corner where she had talked with Midge earlier. "What is it?"

Laura wrung a dustcloth with her hands. "I don't know if I should tell you, but you and Brooke went to dinner with Mr. Waldrin, so I thought you'd want to know."

Faith's pulse raced. "What happened?"

"This morning, Mr. Waldrin went to breakfast for the first time. He usually takes his meals in his room. Anyway, he asked me to have the blankets in his dog's kennel cleaned. They were all muddy, although Mr. Waldrin didn't know how Boomer could have gotten out or where he might have gone."

"Boomer was covered with mud too," Faith said.

"Right. He had taken that cute little dachshund to the pet spa," Laura continued. "When I pulled the dirty blankets out of the kennel, a piece of scrimshaw fell out."

"Can you describe it?" Faith asked. "Maybe it was one of the pieces used to decorate some of the rooms."

"I don't know much about scrimshaw," Laura said, "but this one seemed different. Special. Like some of the costumes I've seen in the guest rooms for the banquet tomorrow night."

Faith nodded. Guests often wore historical costumes to Castleton Manor literary events.

"Most are modern copies of ladies' historical gowns and men's old-fashioned suits, but I can tell others are vintage. They just have that look. Like the scrimshaw. It *feels* old, you know?"

Faith's heart fell. If Milton had hidden the *Essex* scrimshaw in Boomer's kennel, he had to be the murderer. "Where is it now?" Faith asked.

"Since Mr. Waldrin told me to have the blankets cleaned and it was tucked inside them, I thought it would be okay to take it to Marlene."

"So it's in Marlene's office?" Faith could ask Tasi to examine the piece. She might be able to authenticate it or prove it was fake. If it was the *Essex* scrimshaw.

"No, the police took it as evidence."

"And then they took Mr. Waldrin to the station for questioning."

Laura emitted a little squeak, then clapped her hand to her mouth. She glanced around. "I was in a murderer's room?"

"We don't know he's guilty. In fact, I was certain he's not, but after what you told me, the evidence is stacking up against him." Faith thought for a moment. "Do you think you can watch the library while I go talk to someone?"

"I might be able to spare a few minutes, but I'd better get back soon or Ms. Russell won't be too happy."

"I won't be long," Faith promised. "This might be my last chance to get information from this person."

"You have a clue," Laura said. "Do you know who killed Mr. Prather?"

"Not yet."

17

Faith left the library in Laura's capable hands and rushed to the vendors' booths in the nearly empty gallery. Most guests attended the afternoon sessions or were resting in their rooms before dinner. Only a few strolled around the booths.

Faith pretended to browse while she kept her eye on Owen Chase's table. The scrimshander who refused to have a conversation with Faith spoke energetically to a middle-aged couple. His expression was animated. Maybe the prospect of making a sale was enough to turn him from a reticent grump into a gregarious charmer.

Faith looped around tables laden as heavily with wares as they had been on the first day of the conference. The vendors had to be replenishing stock as they sold items, because Faith had seen plenty of guests with shopping bags.

Finally, the couple made a purchase. Owen carefully wrapped a piece of scrimshaw in packing material and placed it in a small paper shopping bag with his store logo printed on the side.

Now was her chance. This might be the last opportunity to question a possible witness, accomplice, or killer.

Faith gathered her courage and marched up to Owen's table.

When Owen spotted Faith, he scowled.

She was ready to give up her quest, but she reached into her pocket and felt the scrimshaw. Milton could be falsely accused of murder, and Owen might have information that could keep the mild-mannered man from going to prison for someone else's crime. "Good afternoon, Mr. Chase."

He grumbled something Faith couldn't quite hear, then focused on making miniscule adjustments to the worktable holding his scrimshaw tools.

Faith had just seen the man smile and chat with customers. She knew he was capable of speech, and she intended to pry a few words out of him. For Milton's sake.

"May I pick your brain for a moment?" Faith asked. "I wondered if you could tell me whether this scrimshaw is a genuine historical piece or a replica. I need an expert's opinion."

An expression flashed across his face that Faith couldn't quite identify. Curiosity? Or annoyance?

"Ordinarily I don't offer free appraisals," he muttered. "But since you're a manor employee, I suppose I can take a quick look."

Owen focused on Faith's hand as she removed the decorative piece from her pocket. Was he hoping Faith had the *Essex* scrimshaw?

She held it out on her palm. The ivory-colored carving nearly covered her small hand.

He reached for it, then seemed to remember his manners and drew back his hand. "May I?" he asked.

"Please," Faith said, handing him the scrimshaw. "I'd like to know whether it's authentic. My cat has been playing with it. Should I be concerned?"

Owen studied it silently, then held a magnifying glass over the carving. "I would estimate it to be no more than twenty years old," he finally said.

Was Faith imagining the disappointment in his voice?

"The material is plastic, possibly with bone meal added," Owen went on. "Some people call it 'fakeshaw.' When endangered species regulations made whale and walrus ivory difficult to acquire, artists were forced to use man-made materials."

"It's just a fake?" Faith had seen the devastated expressions of people on a television antique show when they learned their treasure was a replica, or worse, a deliberate counterfeit. She tried to mimic that now.

"That's a bit harsh." Owen held the scrimshaw under his worktable lamp. "The carving was done by hand. The artist may have been perfecting his or her skills on less expensive materials before carving on a higher quality medium. Ivory is rarely used anymore. You might compare it to the difference between an original painting or a print. This is original art."

"That's a relief," Faith said. "Can scrimshaw be mass produced, like prints?"

"Yes," Owen said. "Poor replicas are turned out in factories for tourist trinkets. You might want to place this out of reach of your cat, because claws and teeth could do serious damage, even to fakeshaw. I would set its value at fifty dollars. Possibly more, due to the fine quality of the engraving."

"Thank you." Faith accepted the piece back from Owen, reluctant to simply toss it into her pocket in front of the knowledgeable scrimshander. He had been helpful. Almost nice.

She hesitated to ask her final question, but there was only one more day of the conference. The vendors would pack up and leave tomorrow. "Do people ever try to pass off fake scrimshaw for the real thing?"

Owen frowned. "That would be highly unethical. Creating replicas is a form of flattery, honoring the early scrimshaw artists. But deliberate deception? No true scrimshander would tolerate the insult to the art form." He turned his attention to his worktable and his back to Faith.

The conversation was over.

Faith did not have time that afternoon to consider the new questions her talk with Owen had generated. She concentrated on work as guests requested her assistance with research or finding the next great novel to read.

When she locked up the library and headed for the cottage, she could finally review the clues that seemed to be accumulating but not leading to any solutions. The many possibilities bounced around her head, nearly making her dizzy.

The *Essex* scrimshaw had never been authenticated. Had Judith been deceived into spending her savings on a replica or even a deliberate fake? If it was real, who had stolen it? Had Raymond been robbed as well as murdered on the dock? Owen was passionate about scrimshaw. Had he been tempted to steal the *Essex* scrimshaw?

Although Faith couldn't be certain he was the man who had been on the dock with Raymond, she had a feeling Owen was involved somehow. He had been avoiding her all week, only speaking to her when she had a piece of scrimshaw she wanted authenticated. He had access to the gallery, and he definitely appeared to have the strength required to throw a harpoon.

The new information didn't make any sense. Had the *Essex* scrimshaw ended up in Boomer's kennel? Had it been buried under the boathouse with the harpoon? Why?

Watson had not been in the cottage when Faith popped in after lunch to pick up the decorative scrimshaw. Tonight he greeted her with a mew and a vigorous ankle rubbing.

Now was the time to find out where he was escaping. Faith changed into her jeans and a favorite sweatshirt and prepared to conduct a thorough search of the cottage.

Her cell phone rang. It was Brooke.

"Do you want to come over for dinner?" Brooke asked.

Faith glanced at Watson. She had an important mission on her evening to-do list. "I wasn't planning to go out," she admitted. "I've already changed into my 'kick around the house' clothes. Mr. Watson Houdini keeps escaping the cottage, and I need to learn his secret."

"This is strictly casual dining," Brooke said. "And you can bring Watson. I have an idea for catching the murderer."

Although Faith had a nagging feeling about Brooke's idea, she agreed.

"Do you want to tag along?" she asked Watson as she grabbed her warm jacket.

The cat scampered to the door.

When they walked to her SUV, a gust of wind scattered leaves across the yard, and she pulled her jacket closer. As soon as Watson had claimed his favorite spot in the passenger seat and she started the engine, she turned the heater to high.

"I don't know what Brooke has in mind," Faith told Watson, "but I don't want her getting into trouble." *Not alone, anyway.*

Faith tried to imagine how Brooke planned to trap a killer as she drove to Lighthouse Bay. She was so involved in her thoughts that she almost didn't notice the car behind her. The curving road was empty of vehicles except for Faith's SUV and a large black sedan.

The car gained on her, following uncomfortably close.

Faith slowed, hoping the car would pass on a straight section of road.

Watson stood on the passenger seat and stared out the rear window at the headlights.

"I know. That driver is being rude."

Watson's whiskers twitched.

Faith glanced in the rearview mirror, nervous about an aggressive driver on such a quiet stretch of road. The headlights were painfully bright. Faith couldn't see the driver or whether there was a passenger. The car might have been a rental driven by a manor guest or an employee heading home after working late.

Finally, the vehicle slowed and dropped back.

Faith kept glancing into her rearview mirror until she reached the well-lit streets of Lighthouse Bay. Instead of driving straight to Brooke's apartment, Faith ambled around side streets until she no longer saw the black sedan.

She felt foolish. The driver obviously had some other destination in mind. Still, when Faith parked at Brooke's building, she was relieved to arrive safely and alone.

Brooke opened the door and welcomed Faith and Watson inside the warm apartment.

"Something smells wonderful," Faith said.

"I'm trying a new recipe for rosemary chicken and a sweet potato dish I might make for my family's Thanksgiving dinner." Brooke had been adopted at an early age by a Massachusetts family. They had nurtured her love of cooking and helped support her when she attended Le Cordon Bleu College of Culinary Arts in Boston. "I need your opinion."

"Of course. I can't wait." Faith loved tasting Brooke's culinary experiments.

They sat at a small table in the kitchen and chatted about everything but murder as they ate the delicious meal.

Watson patiently waited for his own sample, then groomed his face with his paw.

After cleaning up the dishes and putting away leftovers, they moved to the living room and sat on the sofa.

Watson perched on a chair where he had a nice view of the fish tank. He studied the two angelfish as they swam gracefully around the colorful tank.

Faith was glad Watson had enjoyed a treat of chicken. The temptation to try angelfish might be dulled by his full stomach. Not that he had easy access. The tank was sealed with a fluorescent light and hinged cover.

Once they had settled comfortably with cups of herbal tea, Brooke brought up the reason for her invitation—other than seeking Faith's opinion of the scrumptious dinner.

"I waited for you to be here before trying my experiment," Brooke said. "I need a witness. You saw how Diva and Bling reacted when Milton picked us up for dinner Wednesday night."

"Yes. Your fish were definitely upset about something."

Brooke lifted a pink file folder from the coffee table. "I found the brochure for the conference on the manor's website. It included photographs of the speakers." She flipped open the folder. "I printed out pictures of Milton and Rex."

Faith glanced at the computer printouts.

"But first, here's a test." Brooke removed a newspaper clipping from the folder. "This is a photo of a guy that I made the mistake of accompanying to a party at a Boston country club. Diva and Bling tried to warn me about him when he picked me up."

"So what is the test?" Faith asked.

"I want to see if they'll react to a picture the same way they do to phone calls or in-person contact." She showed Faith the clipping.

It was taken from the society page of a Boston newspaper. The large photo featured a handsome man in a tuxedo standing beside a woman in a ball gown. Both held champagne flutes.

Brooke folded the photo to show only the man. She held it close to the fish tank.

Diva and Bling glided past the photo and turned for another pass along the tank's glass wall. Both paused, then began swimming faster. They darted through the water in circles, causing water to splash against the cover.

"That's exactly how they acted when this creep picked me up that awful night," Brooke said. "I should have listened to them." She removed the photo.

Both fish immediately calmed down, resuming a more leisurely swim.

"Just because a man is rich and handsome doesn't mean he's a good catch." Brooke grinned. "But Wolfe is the exception. I'm sure Diva and Bling would love him." She gestured to the cat. "Watson already approves of him."

Faith was used to Brooke teasing her about Wolfe. Brooke insisted that Wolfe had been staying at the manor more often since Faith had started working there. Faith quickly brought them back to the topic at hand. "I'm amazed Diva and Bling can see a photograph through the water and the tank glass."

"They're incredible," Brooke said. "I think we can agree they can spot a creep in a photo. Now let's see if they can identify Raymond's killer."

18

Faith was not entirely convinced the angelfish had such precise radar. But then she reminded herself that some people didn't believe in Watson's detecting skills, even though he had proven himself time and again.

Brooke held Rex's photo to the side of the tank.

The fish swam past with barely a glance.

Faith's heart beat faster as Brooke reached for Milton's photo. She didn't want to believe he was a killer, but what if Diva and Bling reacted? Faith reminded herself to keep an open mind, both concerning Diva and Bling's detective skills and the identity of Raymond's killer.

But the mystery was getting a little too close for comfort. Someone had left a threatening note on Brooke's windshield. Then there was the person sneaking around Faith's cottage and her experience in the garden with a gray-cloaked stalker. And tonight, a car had followed her to Lighthouse Bay. Faith could explain some of the incidents, but they added up to a disturbing sequence of events.

She held her breath when Brooke pressed Milton's photograph against the side of the tank.

Diva and Bling drifted past, their long fins trailing delicately behind them.

"Nothing," Brooke said. "Neither Rex Nelson nor Milton Waldrin can be the killer."

Faith should have felt relieved. Brooke had a lot of confidence in her angelfish, and if they were as accurate as Brooke believed, then Milton was not the murderer. Rex had never been on Faith's suspect list, but no one could be counted out until all the facts were in.

But two other people had stood in the doorway Wednesday night when Diva and Bling went wild.

"It has to be Judith or Agnes." Brooke shrugged. "Case closed."

Faith shook her head. The Lighthouse Bay Police Department would laugh at Faith and Brooke for accusing one of the older women of murder based on the testimony of two angelfish. There had to be some other explanation.

"Isn't the spouse usually the murderer?" Brooke asked.

"You watch too many movies," Faith replied. "Besides, what would Judith's motive be? It can't be money because her family is already wealthy."

"So what about Agnes?"

"Well, she's never been married, and she's always been jealous of Judith's marriage to Raymond."

"Really? How did you find that out?"

"Judith told me after Agnes got angry and marched off." Faith shook her head. "But Agnes walks with a cane. I doubt she could throw a harpoon. Or bury it under the boathouse." Then she remembered Agnes tossing the dog toy down the stairs. Gravity had done most of the work. Hadn't it?

"It's all so confusing. Maybe Diva and Bling reacted because Agnes doesn't like animals. I still think she tried to hit Boomer with her cane on purpose."

"May I see the brochure? I'd like to test your fish on a few more photos."

Brooke released a sigh. "You don't believe them. The brochure is still open on my laptop." She retrieved her computer from another room and set it on the coffee table.

Faith scrolled through the brochure. Maybe the elegant angelfish could confirm whether Owen belonged on the suspect list. She studied every page twice. "There aren't any photos of the vendors. Only images of their shop logos."

"Why do you need them?"

"I spoke to Owen Chase today. Finally. He's been avoiding me. I'm sure he knows something about the murder. And he has a walrus mustache, just like the man on the dock with Raymond."

"There's no photo of him, so we can't test Diva and Bling's detecting skills on him. What about Judith and Agnes?"

"They're attendees, not speakers, so there won't be any photos of them either."

Brooke leaned forward and thumbed through the folder. "Who else are we missing?"

"Glenn Dobie was shoveling rocks onto the foundation of the boathouse Sunday morning," Faith said.

"What motivation would he have to murder Raymond?"

"I don't know, but he could have been burying the murder weapon and scrimshaw." Faith studied the brochure. "There aren't any photos of manor employees."

"Well, we've hit another dead end," Brooke said. "Unless we try to get each of the suspects over here one by one to let Diva and Bling check them out."

"We don't have time. The conference ends tomorrow," Faith reminded her. "Besides, if the suspects figure out what we're doing, the innocent would be insulted and the guilty might come after us."

If the murderer hadn't already figured out Faith and Brooke were trying to learn his or her identity.

Faith let Brooke know she might have been followed to town so her friend could be on the alert, and so that Brooke could let the police know, if something happened to Faith on the way home.

After learning about the huge black sedan, Brooke insisted that Faith spend the night at her house.

Faith declined reluctantly. If Watson missed his breakfast first thing in the morning, Diva and Bling might be too tempting to resist.

Watson was watchful on the ride home. He stayed close to Faith as she walked from her vehicle to the cottage door. Once inside, she called Brooke to let her know they were home safe.

Faith tossed and turned that night, her mind running over the clues and suspects but finding no answers. The deeper she and Brooke dug into the mystery, the more confusing it became.

Watson snuggled against Faith, forcing her to be still. His furry little body rumbled with a soothing purr.

She finally dozed off, thinking all the while that she was missing something important.

Friday morning, Faith left her cottage early. She would need to be alert every minute of the last day of the conference if she hoped to discover who had killed Raymond.

As she walked into the gallery, only a few vendors had arrived to set up for their final day of sales. She walked past the tables belonging to the woman with the ivory comb. Faith's heart sank a little when she noticed the comb was no longer in the display case.

Faith paused when she saw Milton seated on a chair outside the library. At his feet sat Boomer, whose bow tie matched his owner's as usual. Although Brooke believed Diva and Bling had cleared Milton of guilt, Faith wasn't as certain. She regretted arriving so early. In another hour, the now-desolate gallery would be full of vendors and customers.

"Good morning, Mr. Waldrin." Faith tried to keep her voice steady. Whom did she believe: Brooke's pet fish or the police, who had kept Milton at the station for hours the previous day? Then there was the sticky issue of evidence, with most of it pointing toward the man patiently waiting for her.

He nodded, then rose from his chair.

As Faith unlocked the door, she started to ask whether he was enjoying the conference, just to make small talk, but she realized how ridiculous that would sound.

Milton and Boomer followed Faith inside. Boomer's claws made a clicking sound on the wood floor until he stepped onto the plush carpet.

"What brings you to the library so early?" Faith asked. "Is there anything I can help you with?" *Like finding the real murderer so you can prove your innocence? Or would I only be helping you cover up a horrible crime?*

"With all the distractions," Milton said, "I nearly forgot my task to glean first-source information about food choices on a whaling ship. What did the sailors specifically eat?"

Faith wondered at Milton's choice of words. She would have called a man's murder and being swept up in a police investigation far more than distractions.

"The Jaxon family is rumored to have a collection of ship's logs," Milton continued, "yet I've only seen the SS *Honoria* log, which you generously allowed me to study."

She waved a hand toward the Jaxon display case. "The SS *Honoria* wasn't a whaler, but the Jaxons do have more ship logs in their private collection on the third floor. I'm not certain any are from whaling ships or whether they would allow a scholar access."

"Is it possible I might find out?" Milton asked. "It would be a great benefit to my research."

Milton seemed so crestfallen that Faith decided she had to go the extra mile for him. "I'll ask Mr. Jaxon if you can see them."

"Thank you. That would be wonderful."

Faith glanced at the clock on her desk. The Jaxons were early risers, so she typed a text message to Wolfe, hoping he'd silenced his cell phone if he was asleep or otherwise indisposed.

She was surprised to receive a quick answer. She read it, then turned to Milton. "Mr. Jaxon will be down in thirty minutes."

"Oh, thank you. You don't know how much this means to me. After all that's happened . . ." Milton's voice trailed off, and his shoulders slumped.

Boomer gave his owner a doggy smile that seemed to lift Milton's spirits.

"Boomer seems more relaxed," Faith remarked.

At the sound of his name, the dachshund turned in her direction, his tongue lolling out of his mouth and his tail wagging.

"Castleton Manor has been good for Captain Boomer." Milton leaned down to give the dog's long black ears a gentle rub. "He doesn't seem to have been traumatized by his odd adventure. I don't understand how he could have gotten out of his kennel Wednesday night. I'm sure I latched the door, and it's not like Boomer to take off, even if he's allowed the freedom."

Watson had come home that night coated in mud too. Faith had another question, but she needed to phrase it carefully. "I heard Boomer found something interesting while he was out."

Milton looked confused for just a moment, and then he frowned. "You mean that little matter yesterday morning. I have never been so humiliated. How can the police possibly think my Boomer had anything to do with finding that harpoon?" He paused, glancing at the dog sitting at his feet. "Although how he got filthy while inside his kennel is a mystery I have not been able to unravel."

When Milton moved away to study the contents of Tasi's artifact display, Faith hoped she hadn't offended him. It made sense for the police to think Boomer had discovered the harpoon. If that was true, then Watson was involved too.

Milton didn't mention the scrimshaw. Maybe what Laura found in Boomer's kennel wasn't the *Essex* piece. Or maybe it was, and the police were holding back that evidence until they could pin the theft and the murder of Raymond on Milton.

When her cell phone rang, Faith jumped. It was Eileen.

Faith moved behind her desk and sat. "Good morning," she said into the phone.

"Can you talk?" Eileen usually sounded calm, no matter the situation, but now her voice was an excited whisper.

Faith glanced at Milton. He had removed a reprint of a whaling ship log from a shelf and seated himself in front of the fireplace with an open notepad and a pencil.

"I'm at work," she answered.

"You have guests," Eileen said. "I understand. I learned something interesting that might be better told in person. Have you made lunch plans?"

Faith was curious about her aunt's news. "I was just going to eat at home. I'm not needed in the banquet hall until this evening."

"Do you mind if I drop by?"

"That would be wonderful," Faith said. "I have fish chowder leftovers Brooke gave me. It's enough to feed a crowd. Is your information something the rest of the book group would be interested in?"

"Good idea," Eileen said. "I'll bring a salad. See you at noon."

Faith called Midge and Brooke. As she'd expected, Brooke had to work through lunch, but Midge was available.

"What's this all about?" Midge asked.

"I don't know," Faith said. "We'll both find out at lunch."

"Can I bring something from Snickerdoodles?" Midge asked.

"Eileen is bringing salad, and I have fish chowder."

"It sounds like corn muffins would fit in nicely."

Wolfe arrived shortly after Faith finished her phone calls. As usual, he was dressed impeccably in a tailored suit and a tie. His warm smile never failed to brighten Faith's day.

She nodded toward the fireplace. "Mr. Waldrin and Boomer are ready to see your collection."

The men exchanged pleasantries, then headed toward the library door.

Wolfe paused just before they left and faced Faith. "I haven't had a chance to talk to you since Wednesday."

"The conference has kept us all busy," Faith said, hoping her comment didn't sound as lame to Wolfe as it did to her.

"Do you have a costume for the banquet tonight?" he asked.

Because Faith was a conference speaker, she knew she was expected to attend the final banquet Friday night. But in costume? She spluttered something along the lines that she had not entertained the idea and doubted her wardrobe contained whaling-era garb.

Wolfe laughed. "No, I imagine not." He glanced at Milton and Boomer, waiting patiently in the doorway. "I'll drop by later."

At noon, guests vacated the library and gallery, and they headed for the banquet hall and a lunch that was certain to be delicious.

Faith locked the library, bundled up in her coat and scarf, and walked to her cottage for her own delicious lunch.

Watson was perched in a window. When he saw Faith, he hopped down.

Faith opened the door a crack, but the cat made no attempt to escape. He simply sat on the carpet and stared at her.

"Did your bath convince you to stay home?" Faith scratched Watson behind the ears. "Or are you just being more careful to conceal your escapades from me?"

He blinked at Faith.

That might mean a yes to either question, or it might mean nothing at all. There was no telling with her cat. Faith suspected not much could keep Watson home if he wanted to go on an adventure. Not even Marlene's order that he stay out of the manor until Agnes left.

Faith didn't have time to hunt for his escape route because she heard a knock on the cottage door. When she answered, she found Eileen and Midge standing there. Both had brought their contributions for lunch.

"How are you?" Midge asked the cat. She lifted Watson into her arms and looked him over. "In my expert opinion, you are in excellent health."

Watson mewed, then snuggled against Midge and purred. He loved Midge—as long as she wasn't giving him an exam or a vaccination.

Soon the cat wriggled out of Midge's arms and jumped to the floor. He took up his spot on the back of the sofa to gaze out the window.

After heating the chowder and muffins, they sat at the kitchen table. No one spoke for a few minutes, other than to rhapsodize about the wonderful flavors.

Eileen dabbed her mouth with a cloth napkin. "You're probably wondering what was so important that I asked you to meet on such short notice."

"I'm pretty sure it isn't to announce the next reading selection for the book club," Midge responded.

"You're right. I was curious about something Faith said, and I did a little research." Eileen opened a pocket on the front of her knitting bag and extracted a sheet of paper. Without a word, she handed it to her niece.

Faith read aloud, "The headline says, 'Local Woman Headed to Track-and-Field Olympic Trials.'" She examined the photo of a young woman in her early twenties. "This is definitely Agnes. 'Miss VanStuth will represent the United States in—'" Faith stopped, stunned.

"What is it?" Midge peeked over Faith's shoulder.

Faith stared at the other two women. "Agnes nearly went to the Olympics due to her javelin-throwing skill."

19

Eileen wore a pained expression, clearly unhappy to have discovered evidence potentially damaging to Agnes. "I wouldn't condemn a person based solely on a newspaper article, but this is an interesting development."

Midge nodded. "I know what it's like to be falsely accused of a crime. We can't jump to conclusions just because things look bad for Agnes."

"Her legs were broken in the bus accident, and she walks with a cane," Faith pointed out. "She might have been strong when she was a young woman, but now she seems frail."

"But that doesn't mean she can't throw a harpoon," Midge said. "I've seen it in pets who lose a limb due to disease or an accident. Their other limbs develop to compensate for the missing leg. Agnes might have weak legs, but her upper-body strength could be as good or better than when she was in her early twenties."

"That's the problem." Faith sighed. "More than a strong throwing arm was needed to commit the murder. The killer had to carry that harpoon from the gallery, hike or drive to the boathouse, and take a motorboat across choppy waters to Lighthouse Bay."

"We now know Agnes might be capable of throwing the harpoon," Midge said. "Who else is there?"

"Milton was taken in for questioning by the police," Faith answered. "They must consider him a prime suspect. Tasi seems strong enough to throw a harpoon, and she's knowledgeable about all things having to do with whaling. Both Milton and Tasi had an argument with Raymond shortly before his murder. Of course, there's Judith, Raymond's widow. And then there's Owen Chase, the scrimshander."

"I haven't heard about him," Eileen said.

Faith told them about her conversation with Owen the previous afternoon, then later that evening, the car following her to town when she went to Brooke's for dinner.

"The driver was probably just going the same way as me," Faith concluded. "Once I reached Lighthouse Bay, it stopped following me."

"I don't like the sound of that," Eileen said. "I'm glad the conference ends tonight."

"That's good but also bad," Midge commented. "Once everyone leaves town, the police will have a harder time figuring out who killed Raymond."

Eileen touched Faith's arm. "I hope you'll stay put tonight. No more sleuthing. Let the police handle this."

"I have to attend the final banquet," Faith said. "Wolfe specifically reminded me this morning that he expects me to be there."

"First, dinner at The Captain's Table," Midge teased, "and now he requests your presence at a banquet?"

"It's not like that," Faith insisted. "The Captain's Table was pure chance, and the banquet is related to work. Brooke will be in the kitchen, and I'll be surrounded by manor employees and conference guests. I'll be safe there tonight."

Midge shivered. "Until the murderer is caught, are any of us safe?"

A knock on the front door made all three women jump.

Watson hopped off the back of the sofa and trotted to the foyer.

Faith followed, glancing back at the two women.

"We've got your back," Midge whispered.

Faith opened the door.

Charlotte Jaxon stood on the front step, an enormous dress box balanced across her arms, and smiled. "Wolfe thought you might need this."

"Thank you." Faith took the box from Charlotte and invited her inside.

Eileen and Midge came through the kitchen doorway as Charlotte walked into the living room. They exchanged greetings while Faith set the box on the coffee table.

"My son is on a conference call." Charlotte bent to rub Watson behind the ears. "He asked me to bring this by."

"Wolfe said something about wearing costumes for the banquet." Faith pointed at the box. "Is that for tonight?"

Charlotte nodded. "I found it in the attic. The dress belonged to a Jaxon woman and dates to the mid-1800s."

"Oh, what fun!" Midge exclaimed. "May we see?"

"Of course," Charlotte replied. "If you'll do the honors, Faith?"

Faith gasped when she lifted the lid. Resting on top of acres of sky-blue fabric and cream lace was a corset. Under the dress was a contraption that had to be a hoopskirt frame.

"You must wear this too." Charlotte reached into her coat pocket and removed a velvet jewelry box. She handed it to Faith. "Wolfe gave it to me to wear with my costume, but it doesn't go with my dress. I'm loaning it to you for the evening."

Faith opened the jewelry box. Inside rested the ivory comb with the delicate intertwined roses.

Midge and Eileen murmured their approval.

"It will go perfectly with the dress," Charlotte said. "They're a matched set."

Wolfe had bought the comb for his mother after all. Faith was glad it hadn't gone to a conference attendee, who would take the comb away forever.

Overwhelmed, Faith sat down heavily on a cushioned chair. "Thank you so much. Your generosity takes my breath away," she told Charlotte.

Charlotte waved off her gratitude. "Think nothing of it. It's about time that dress was put to good use."

"What is it, dear?" Eileen asked, noticing Faith's expression of consternation.

"Well, it's just . . . I don't know how to put on a dress like this," Faith admitted.

"I'll come back to help you tonight," Midge offered, slipping into her Southern accent. "I've helped dozens of women with their costumes for Civil War reenactment events. I know all about hoopskirts."

"That would be great," Faith told her. "How long will it take?"

"We'll need at least an hour. Two would be better."

Faith tried to focus on work that afternoon and not the prospect of receiving a whaling-era makeover. Guests crowded the library between sessions, browsing the shelves and returning books. They seemed to be enjoying their last afternoon in the manor.

She was checking in reference materials from three historians when Wolfe entered the library.

As the guests picked up their conference bags, one of them said, "We'll just have time to change for dinner."

More costumes, Faith suspected. She'd need to get going soon to make sure she had time to get into her own costume, but for now she smiled at Wolfe. "Did Milton find what he needed in your collection?"

"Yes. He took copious notes while I was on a conference call in my office. He was delighted when I told him he could scan the illustrations."

"At least he can leave the manor on a happy note," Faith commented.

"I heard the police questioned him," Wolfe said. "I can't believe Milton is a murderer. But if he isn't, that means someone else is here with blood on their hands."

Faith wondered who that might be if it wasn't Milton. Owen the scrimshander? Tasi Kekoa? Glenn Dobie? Judith Prather? Agnes VanStuth? Faith must have looked as queasy as she felt, because Wolfe rested a steadying hand on her shoulder.

"I've hired extra security tonight," he said in a confidential tone. "They'll be dressed as waitstaff, so no one will notice."

"Is there a reason for the added security?" *Like a threat?*

"No, nothing specific," Wolfe answered. "Maybe I'm being too cautious, but I can't take a chance on anyone getting hurt. I also don't want anything ruining the last night of the conference. The organizers are already talking about scheduling another one at Castleton next year, despite Mr. Prather's unfortunate demise."

Faith had noticed that some guests enjoyed the macabre thrill of murder and mayhem in their midst as long as it didn't touch them personally. Far from destroying Castleton Manor's reputation, as Marlene feared, the mysteries seemed to be part of the draw.

"I heard the harpoon was found," Faith said. "And that Milton's dachshund might have been the one to dig it up."

"Yes. That's why the police took Milton in for questioning. Apparently, the harpoon and the dachshund were both covered with mud."

Faith hesitated. The owner of the manor deserved to know about an employee's potential involvement in a crime affecting his business. Or that of the employee's animal companion. "Boomer wasn't the only animal coated with mud that night."

"Oh?"

Faith took a deep breath. "On Wednesday night, I know I locked Watson inside the cottage when I left, but when I came home, he was outdoors and covered in mud. I had to give him a bath."

"That's strange."

Faith plunged ahead, hoping Wolfe wasn't going to laugh at her theory. "I think Watson let Boomer out of his kennel, and they dug up the harpoon together. They've been really chummy. Milton had nothing to do with it, because he was at dinner with us at the time."

Wolfe raised his eyebrows. "I agree that Watson has an uncanny ability to sniff out clues, but sneaking a dog out of his kennel, digging up a murder weapon, and returning the dog to the kennel might be beyond even Watson's impressive skills. And this doesn't let Milton off the hook."

"Why not?" Faith asked.

"He might have buried the harpoon days before our dinner at The Captain's Table."

Faith puzzled over the sequence of events, trying to fit them together. "Maybe Boomer remembered helping Milton bury the harpoon. Then he took Watson with him to dig it up." She frowned. "Although that doesn't make sense. Why would he do that? Unless Milton accidentally buried the *Essex* scrimshaw with the harpoon. Maybe he went back for it after dinner Wednesday night. But the timing isn't right."

"We should let the police handle the mystery," Wolfe said. "We have other business to attend to. Speaking of, did my mother bring you the costume?"

"Yes, thank you," Faith said. "Midge is going to help me put it on. Please tell me I won't be the only one at the banquet in costume."

Wolfe smiled. "Absolutely not. Mother and I are both dressing up."

The cat had witnessed bustling activity in the manor basement many times. As he sat outside the massive kitchen, savoring wonderful cooking smells, he knew what was coming. The humans had one last feast at the end of their events. Maybe they had to eat all the food that was left so it would not spoil. If they would just listen, he could have told them that there would be a new crowd of humans arriving in a few days. The manor was never quiet for long.

That meant his friend would soon be leaving. The cat had never imagined he could become so attached to a dog. Unfortunately, they had failed to spot a whale. The cat could continue his quest at hi leisure, but the canine might not have access to the sea at his home. He certainly did not have a friend willing to spring him free from his cage to go on adventures.

The cat ran upstairs, pausing when he reached the lobby. He watched for the human with the cane. It seemed wise to avoid being seen by her.

Arriving safely on the second floor, the cat moved along one wall toward the door of the Persian cat. He detected movement and heard her human's voice. The Persian must have been preparing to attend the feast. There was no sense trying to free the dog now when humans were milling around the halls.

He waited beside the Persian's door, patient as his kind could be when there was a goal in mind.

Finally, the door opened.

The cat stood squarely in the way, hoping the human would pause long enough for him to gaze upon the fluffy beauty securely in her arms.

"Hello, kitty," the human said. She knelt to give him a pat on the head. The human wore what appeared to be a cape made from birds. But the feathers were not real.

His heart fluttered in his throat as the Persian deigned to look his way. He stretched his neck, his whiskers alert and his nose catching every perfumed scent.

She seemed startled at first, then leaned down. They touched noses briefly.

Another person walked toward them.

The Persian's human stood, her long skirt brushing against him as she turned. "Mr. Waldrin, you dressed the part of a whaling captain. Where did you find a period jacket in such good condition?"

"My sister is a seamstress," the other person said. "Your costume is quite lovely, if you don't mind me making the observation."

Their voices were friendly, and the cat expected them to touch noses any moment now in a gesture of affection.

"The print is authentic," she said. "A reproduction of a fabric in an

old photograph. But the dress is cut more modestly, and the shawl makes the lightweight cotton bearable in this New England chilly weather."

"Are those real feathers?"

They chattered like two birds as they strolled toward the stairs.

The cat followed, hopeful that he could sit near the long-haired queen of the banquet.

"Where is your handsome companion tonight?" the Persian's human asked.

"Captain Boomer doesn't like crowds," he said. "He's staying in our room. Normally, I don't enjoy crowds either, but I would be delighted to sit next to you during the banquet."

The cat abandoned his plan. The dog was alone in his room. That was no way to spend his last evening at the manor.

Not when there were more interesting things to do.

When Faith entered her cottage, Watson was gone. "Rumpy, you scamp," she said to an empty house.

Soon the conference would end, and she would have time to find Watson's escape route. Faith didn't have long to ponder ways to keep her cat safe inside the cottage because Midge arrived, carrying a bag full of hair-care items and makeup.

"Do we really need all that?" Faith protested, eyeing it with distrust.

"Yes, we do." Midge lifted a bag of ribbons. "I hope I have a color match here."

Faith led the way to her bedroom.

First, Midge separated Faith's long chestnut hair into two sections. The top she worked into a thick braid, weaving a cream-colored ribbon into the plait. Midge inserted the ivory comb in the middle of the coiled braid so that it resembled a little crown. Using a curling iron, Midge gave Faith a dozen ringlets in the lower section of her hair.

Faith studied Midge's handiwork in the mirror. "This is amazing. But I admit I feel ridiculous."

"You won't once you see it with the dress." Midge smiled. "You'll look like a fairy princess from every little girl's dream."

The corset was the first hurdle, and it wasn't as bad as Faith had expected.

"I intentionally left it loose," Midge explained. "You'll need some room for the banquet food. Traditionally, you'd have precious little room to breathe, much less eat."

The hoop frame was an engineering marvel. Midge fastened it around Faith's waist. Next, the dress went over Faith's head. She was lost in a sea of crinkling blue fabric as Midge tugged it carefully over her styled hair. Finally, Midge fastened the dozens of tiny buttons using a special hook.

"Most dresses from this era are tiny," Midge said. "I've seen authentic period dresses for grown women that would barely fit a modern child. You're lucky the Jaxon women were tall and healthy, and that you're so slender. I'll only need to take a couple of tucks here and there."

Off came the dress again, and Midge basted in a few temporary darts.

Once Faith had the entire costume on, she barely recognized herself in the full-length mirror. She would have loved being dressed up like this when she was a young girl.

"I don't exactly look like a librarian. If this wasn't my last chance to find Raymond's killer, I would beg out of attending the banquet." Faith wiggled her toes. "What about shoes?"

Midge rustled around in the tissue-lined dress box. "There's nothing here. But don't worry. Any simple flats or slippers will do. No one's going to see your feet."

Faith scanned her closet, then pointed to a pair of suitable shoes. "Could you grab the cream-colored flats there? I can't exactly bend over right now."

Midge chuckled, retrieved the shoes, and set them in front of her friend.

Faith lifted her formidable skirts and stepped into the shoes, then regarded herself in the mirror again. "Thank you. I would have never been able to do all this myself."

"Now you see why people love wearing clothes from other eras," Midge said. "Especially this style. I have a hoop dress in my closet for special occasions."

"I wish you were wearing it now and accompanying me to the banquet." Faith thought of something. "Oh no!"

"What?" Midge asked, checking the dress and Faith's hair for problems.

"How am I going to get up and down stairs?" Faith asked.

"Very carefully," Midge said with a grin. "I'll walk with you to the manor."

The trip along the paved walk to the manor took longer than usual. Thankfully, there were no gusts of wind. Midge escorted Faith up the wide marble steps, into the manor, and to the doorway of the banquet hall.

"You're not the only one in costume," Midge whispered.

Faith glanced around the room. Nearly everyone was dressed in period attire. Ship's captains and sailors, gentlemen and ladies, shopkeepers and workmen all served to transform the banquet hall into a scene from a long-ago era.

She saw Wolfe and Charlotte sitting together at a table. Charlotte noticed Faith and waved her over.

"Knock 'em dead." Midge gave Faith a little nudge.

When Wolfe glanced up and smiled, Faith thought maybe the time spent dressing had been worth it.

He rose from his seat and bowed. His captain's dress jacket, with rows of brass buttons and long tails, was tailored to his athletic physique. "You look lovely, my lady."

Faith gave a little curtsy. "Why thank you, Captain Jaxon."

Charlotte was resplendent in a velvet gown in a soft shade of rose, her dark brown hair in an elaborate bun at the back of her head. She stood, appearing perfectly comfortable and graceful in the floor-length gown. "I would prefer you sat at our table, but your presence has been requested by Mr. Waldrin."

Faith shot a worried glance at Wolfe.

He nodded subtly toward a man placing shrimp cocktail in front of diners.

Faith didn't recognize him or two other servers. She remembered Wolfe telling her that he had beefed up security for the night, and she smiled at him gratefully.

Wolfe offered his arm. "I'll see you to your table. Perhaps you might be so kind as to save room on your dance card for me?"

People are going to dance in these costumes? Then Faith realized he must be joking with her. Here she was, ready to put all kinds of meaning into a harmless little quip. "You may certainly count on a prominent spot on my dance card."

"Excellent." Wolfe pulled out a chair at a round table for Faith. Milton, Tasi, and Rex, each dressed in period attire, were seated at the table along with four other guests. "Captain Waldrin, sir, I turn Miss Newberry over to your capable charge."

Faith blanched at the thought of sitting down in the hoopskirt. She watched a woman in similar attire take her seat at the next table and tried to imitate her method of tucking and arranging the skirt. She managed to get it done without disaster.

Wolfe bowed, and as he walked away, Faith realized she was dining with two of her murder suspects.

As she greeted her companions for the evening, Faith surreptitiously looked for the other suspects. The banquet was part of the conference package, but tickets could be purchased by anyone interested in the evening's speaker and the sumptuous meal. Owen sat at a table by the doors with other vendors. Judith and Agnes were at a table near the dais where a podium stood with a microphone attached for the speaker.

After the appetizers had been cleared and the salads served, the conference director went to the mic. He thanked various people for their assistance in coordinating the event and announced that the New England Whaling in History and Literature Conference planned to meet at Castleton Manor again next year.

The audience applauded, approving a return to the manor.

Next, the director introduced Judith Prather and motioned her forward.

She rose. Her gray wool jacket and floor-length matching skirt were drab, but they gave her a dated prim look that fit in with the costumes worn by the other guests and staff. She climbed the steps to the dais and stood beside the podium.

As the conference director eulogized Raymond and listed his accomplishments, Judith wiped away tears.

"And now I'd like to make another exciting announcement," the director continued. "The conference committee seeks to honor Raymond's many contributions to the study of scrimshaw art and his conservation of significant historical pieces. Therefore, a donation to the conference scholarship fund will be made in Raymond Prather's name to assist a worthy student in pursuing the study of the whaling era."

While the audience clapped, the conference director handed Judith a plaque, and they posed for a photograph. The director gestured toward the mic, but Judith shook her head and headed for the steps.

Seated next to Faith, Rex dabbed his napkin to each eye briefly. "Very moving."

Two ladies at their table murmured their agreement.

"I'm not surprised she didn't give a speech," one said. "Poor Mrs. Prather lost her husband only a week ago."

Faith turned her attention to the next speaker as the salads were removed and the main course set in front of the guests—tender sea bass fillets served on a bed of delicate greens and drizzled with a flavorful beurre blanc sauce. Mouthwatering duchess potatoes accompanied the fish.

By the time the main speaker rose to the dais, the diners were sipping coffee and enjoying dessert in the form of a dainty cup of custard flavored with vanilla and raspberry coulis. The rich food made Faith drowsy, and she noticed there were a few others in the crowd who felt the same way.

The lights dimmed, and a slide show was projected on the wall. A talk about the excavation of the sunken whaling ship *Belle Marie* off the coast of Maine should have been exciting, but the professor spoke in a dry monotone. Photos of the seafloor showed bits of protruding ship.

Most of the audience seemed enthralled to hear what must have been the highlight of the entire week, but Faith could not make sense of it and found her attention wandering.

She watched Judith stand and slip through the door. Faith thought the woman was probably taking a restroom break. Faith would have too, if she hadn't been afraid of how to manage the hoopskirt in a bathroom stall.

A few minutes later, Milton's cell phone chirped. Faith watched as he studied the glowing face of the phone, then rose abruptly.

First Judith, now Milton. Faith wanted to follow, but she would be too obvious, bolting out of the room after the two. Especially in a sky-blue vintage gown.

Brooke made her way between the tables, stopping beside Faith. She stooped to whisper, "Judith just stormed out of the manor."

Faith imagined Judith suddenly packing up and leaving. She glanced around the table and was surprised to see faces hungry for a scrap of gossip. She carefully stood and led Brooke to the empty corridor.

Brooke looked Faith up and down. "Wow, that dress is amazing. And your hair is gorgeous."

Faith patted the bodice of the gown. "The outfit is courtesy of Charlotte, and Midge dressed me." She waited for a guest to pass by, then leaned close to Brooke and whispered, "Judith checked out?"

"I came upstairs to help bring the dessert dishes to the kitchen so the staff can finish cleaning and go home before it snows tonight. Judith rushed down this very corridor at breakneck speed."

"How do you know she left the manor?" Faith asked.

A guest exited the banquet hall as another guest returned, passing Faith and Brooke.

"We can't talk here," Faith said.

They walked to the lobby and stood beside a forest of tall potted palms.

"I followed Judith," Brooke said. "If she was going to her room at that speed, I was afraid she might be ill. With everything else that's gone on this week, I didn't want the manor accused of a case of food poisoning."

Faith nodded.

"But she didn't go to the elevator or the stairs or the front entrance. She left the building through one of the French doors in the gallery."

"A few minutes after she left the banquet, Milton glanced at his phone," Faith told her. "Without saying a word to anyone at our table, he rushed out."

"This has to involve Raymond's murder," Brooke said.

"Or the *Essex* scrimshaw."

Brooke shrugged. "How can we find out? I have to get back to the kitchen—"

Movement on the stairs caught Faith's eye. She grabbed Brooke's sleeve and dragged her behind the palms.

Milton hurried down the carpeted stairs, his heavy wool coat buttoned securely. He stopped at the front desk and handed the clerk an envelope. Then he exited through the main doors.

Faith moved from behind the potted palms and rushed to the desk. "I need to see that envelope," she told the night clerk.

"Mr. Waldrin said not to open it unless he doesn't return."

"We need to make sure he returns," Brooke said. "Hand over the note!"

The startled clerk let Faith snatch the envelope from his hand. She tore it open.

I am meeting Judith Prather on the Castleton Manor private dock. If I do not return, question Mrs. Prather. She

claims to know the location of the Essex scrimshaw. I suspect
she has something else in mind, and I intend to stop her.

He also included his sister's contact information and instructions for Boomer's care.

Faith was surprised that Milton was going after Judith. Apparently, he wasn't as timid as he appeared.

Brooke took the note from Faith and scanned it. "We have to follow them."

"I need to call Wolfe first. He hired extra security staff for tonight." Faith grabbed her phone out of the period reticule she carried and placed the call. Wolfe didn't answer, so she left him a brief voice mail.

"I hope he checks his messages soon," Brooke remarked.

"How can I chase anyone in this?" Faith patted the hoopskirt. "I can't possibly hike to the cliffs."

"There's a road to the boathouse. We'll go in my car. Wait out front, and I'll pick you up."

The cat had to work more than his usual tricks, but soon he and the dog were racing out on the dock. This was his friend's last chance for whale watching.

He wished he had been able to figure out how to cloak himself in one of the dog's little coats. The wind gusted, dusting his whiskers with snowflakes. Maybe this hadn't been such a good idea.

Then the dog lifted his long muzzle, his nose twitching.

Two humans came down the steps from the cottage on the hill. One was the canine's human. The other one was female.

The cat ducked behind a wooden box that smelled like the sea—briny, fishy, and delicious.

"You stole the Essex scrimshaw from my husband," the female human said.

"The police as much as accused me of the same thing," the dog's person said, *"but I did no such thing."*

"I want it back!"

"Then I suggest you speak to the local police," the dog's human replied calmly.

The woman screamed and lunged at the dog's human.

The dog dashed out of their hiding place, barking ferociously.

A light in the boathouse keeper's cottage winked on as Faith and Brooke pulled into the small parking lot that served the boathouse. Faith briefly thought of stopping to recruit Glenn's assistance, but Milton might not have time. In his note, the man had sounded determined to confront Judith. Unless he was the thief and murderer. Faith still hadn't figured it out, but at least her list of suspects had been narrowed down.

"You have to be prepared for New England weather." Brooke opened the trunk. "You'll need this." She handed Faith a fleece-lined windbreaker, then pulled a heavy sweatshirt over her white chef's coat.

"You're a lifesaver." Faith put on the windbreaker, but she couldn't zip it up over the hoopskirt.

Faith led Brooke along the side of the cottage to the steps to the boathouse, then let her take the lead. Brooke could move faster than Faith, whose gown was designed for appearance, not functionality. When they heard a dog bark, Faith struggled to hurry.

Behind them, they heard a vehicle come to a gravel-scattering halt in the parking lot. A car door slammed.

"I think Wolfe took my call seriously," Faith told Brooke. "That must be the security guards."

"Should we wait for them?" Brooke asked.

"They'll have no trouble catching up."

The dress hindered Faith's movements, so Brooke offered her a hand on a steep section of the walkway.

As they neared the boathouse, a man caught up with them, his breath coming out in frozen puffs.

Faith's relief was quickly replaced by terror when she realized he was not one of Wolfe's security guards. The man resembled a sailor in one of the paintings displayed in the manor. He was dressed in a heavy peacoat, boots, and buckskin trousers, and he had a thick walrus mustache.

It was Owen.

21

Owen Chase had been on Faith's list of murder suspects. Now here he was, ready to kill her and Brooke and maybe Judith and Milton too.

As her mind clouded with panic, Faith wondered where Owen planned to dispose of their bodies. He wouldn't bury them under the boathouse, because the police already knew about that hiding place.

"Hold on there, mister." Brooke groped under her sweatshirt for the pocket of her white chef's coat. She pulled out a little paring knife that might have been dangerous to potatoes and carrots, but it hardly posed a threat to the scrimshander.

"What are you doing here?" Faith demanded.

"The same as you, I expect," Owen replied. "Judith sent me a message. She said she knew where the *Essex* scrimshaw is. I came to see for myself. Do you have it?" He took a step toward them.

Brooke waved the tiny knife. "Stay back."

"We don't have the *Essex* scrimshaw," Faith said.

Then Faith heard voices near the boathouse. She and Brooke were sandwiched between potential murderers. If Wolfe hadn't sent the police or at least a security guard, they were sunk deeper than the *Belle Marie*.

"Didn't you think meeting Judith on a dock at night was fishy?" Brooke asked.

"Or repetitious," Faith said. "You were on the north dock. You killed Raymond."

"No! I was standing next to him when the—when he was killed."

Owen might not have been the person who threw the harpoon, but he still might have been involved in his murder somehow. "You were there to steal the *Essex* scrimshaw," Faith accused.

"Now why would I do that?" Owen smirked. "I had access to it a month ago."

"What are you talking about?" Brooke asked.

"Raymond Prather hired me to make a duplicate of the *Essex* scrimshaw," Owen explained. "At first, I was delighted to use my talents to re-create such a historical piece. But then I realized I was being pulled into a scam. I was on the dock that night to tell Raymond I wouldn't complete the copy for him."

"What scam?" Faith asked. "People make replicas of historic scrimshaw. There's nothing wrong with that. You told me so yourself."

"It's wrong when a man does it to steal from his own wife," Owen said. "Raymond hired me to create the replica. I was shocked when he offered to sell me the original. His intention was to pocket the money and pass off the *Essex* copy to his wife as the real thing."

"If your intentions are so honorable, why are you using a fake name?" Faith asked. "I know Owen Chase was the first mate on the *Essex*."

Owen grinned. "Owen Chase is my real name. My parents are whaling-era enthusiasts too. Where do you think I got my love for it? With their last name being Chase, they saw an opportunity when I was born, and they took it."

"Oh. I'm sorry," Faith said, feeling more than a little embarrassed.

"Don't worry. I get that a lot."

Brooke nudged Faith and pointed to the top of the cliff near Glenn's cottage, where Faith caught a glimpse of flashing red and blue lights. She focused on Owen as he continued his explanation.

"Raymond planned to have a Boston antiquities expert verify the original scrimshaw, then switch it with the replica. He would sell the original to me or to some unscrupulous private collector."

"So you have the *Essex* scrimshaw?" Brooke lowered her knife. "Or the copy?"

"Only the partially completed replica." Owen shook his head. "I couldn't afford to purchase a piece that rare and valuable. I thought

I'd lost it for good when Raymond was murdered and it went missing. Then Judith sent me that message. I thought perhaps she had found it. Maybe she had it all along and was going to double dip by both selling it to a collector and cashing in on an insurance policy by claiming it was stolen. I can't allow the *Essex* scrimshaw to pass into obscurity in a private collection, never to be enjoyed by historians and students. I came here to talk her into donating it to a museum."

"Judith doesn't have the scrimshaw," Faith said. "The police do."

"Thank heaven for little blessings." Owen looked genuinely relieved. "Then why did Judith want to meet?"

They heard a dog bark out on the dock, then human voices raised in anger.

While the dog's human and the woman shouted at each other, the cat saw his human sneak behind the boathouse. The wind tugged at her bell-shaped skirt. He'd seen sails on boats in summertime do the same thing. He feared she might be blown away. Between the weather and the arguing humans, the dock was a dangerous place to be, and he wanted his human to leave.

The cat meowed, but his human didn't understand. Maybe she couldn't hear him over the howling wind.

He hopped down from his perch, lowered his body into stalking mode, and crept closer to the angry humans and barking dog. The only way he could rescue his human was by working his way around the fight.

Faith, Brooke, and Owen followed the voices and hid behind the boathouse. Faith and Brooke huddled close together as they peeked out from behind a corner of the building. Snowflakes slapped Faith's face, the cold stinging her cheeks. She wanted nothing more than to retreat to her cozy cottage.

Then she spotted Watson on the dock. Snow clung to his fur, and soon the black sections of his tuxedo markings would match his white paws and face.

His dachshund friend bounced around Judith's ankles, as though deciding which one to nip first, a low growl rumbling in his throat. Boomer didn't wear a coat or a bow tie. Milton had left him at the manor, according to the note he had given the desk clerk. So how had the dog ended up on the dock?

"Tell your hound to back off," Judith ordered Milton.

"Boomer was in my room, locked in his kennel," Milton said. "I have no idea how he got here, but I'm beginning to suspect you've been sneaking into my room. You must have let him out Wednesday night. How did he get muddy? What did you do to him?"

Judith, whom Faith had initially considered refined, snorted. "Don't be ridiculous. Why would I bother with your dog, much less let him out of a cage, where he clearly belongs? You dug up the crown jewel of my collection, you thief!"

Milton was silent for a moment. The police must not have told him about the scrimshaw Laura had found in Boomer's kennel.

Realization dawned, and Faith grabbed Brooke's arm. "Only the person who hid the harpoon would know a piece of scrimshaw was buried with it," she whispered.

"And only the killer would hide the murder weapon," Brooke whispered back. "Diva and Bling were right."

"Who are Diva and Bling?" Owen asked.

Milton interrupted their hushed conversation. "What are you talking about?" he asked Judith. "The only things in Boomer's kennel were blankets and toys."

"Where is it?" Judith screamed at Milton. "Give me back the *Essex* scrimshaw!"

"I don't have it!" Milton shouted. "That's why I came here. You claimed you had it."

"And you came because you wanted to make sure you had the authentic piece."

"That's not true," Milton protested.

"Everyone in the manor talked about your muddy dog and your visit with the police. That creature dug up the *Essex* scrimshaw."

Boomer crouched low on the dock, growling and showing his teeth.

Faith didn't know whether it was her cat's influence or the fact that his owner was in danger, but there was no sign of the shy, fearful puppy she had grown used to seeing.

"So that's how Boomer got so muddy," Milton said. "He really did dig up the harpoon. But I don't know anything about the scrimshaw. How do you know it was with the harpoon?"

Judith folded her arms across her chest. "Because I buried it."

Faith exchanged startled glances with Brooke.

"You buried the *Essex* scrimshaw?" Milton sounded genuinely baffled. "It's worth a fortune."

"The real one is," Judith said.

"What do you mean?" Milton still sounded puzzled.

"I discovered Raymond was purchasing fake scrimshaw with my money. He gave me cheap fakes and pocketed the rest of the money. I imagine he planned to drain my fortune and leave me with nothing but a collection of junk, then walk out on me."

Milton remained silent. He appeared shocked at the news.

"I hoped to recover money from the insurance company for the loss of the phony *Essex* scrimshaw." Judith glared at Milton. "But then your wretched dog dug it up and ruined my plan."

"You killed Raymond with the harpoon," Milton said. "And you lured me here, hoping to get a fake back so you could defraud your insurance company?"

"That was the idea." Judith sighed. "But just like your dog, you've gone and ruined everything. I can't let you live now that you know the truth."

"No!" Agnes suddenly appeared, hobbling toward Judith and leaning heavily on her cane. She stopped in front of her sister and glowered. "Don't you dare hurt anyone else."

"You are in no position to tell me what to do," Judith spat, then snatched the ivory-handled cane right out of Agnes's hand.

The swift movement caused Agnes to lose her balance, and she fell.

Clutching the cane like a baseball bat, Judith turned and swung it at Milton.

He ducked.

The dock was slippery with newly fallen snow and salty spray. Both Judith and Milton tottered around in a slow-motion battle, their feet sliding, which might have been comical if not for Judith's deadly intentions.

Owen brushed past Faith and Brooke as he left their hiding place. He dashed onto the dock, his boots skidding. "The *Essex* scrimshaw the dog dug up is real!"

Judith whirled around. "It is?"

Owen nodded as he took a few steps closer to Judith. "Your husband paid me to make a copy. When I realized what he was doing, I met him on the dock, hoping to talk some sense into him. Instead, that harpoon plunged through him. Your *Essex* scrimshaw is safe. It's in the hands of the police now."

"Why didn't you tell me?" Judith screamed. She swung the cane at him.

There was a sharp crack as the cane connected with Owen's head, and he dropped to the dock like a sack of potatoes.

Judith turned to Milton and took another violent swipe at him.

But Milton moved out of the way. The man was proving he could be scrappy when push came to shove.

"Thank goodness!" Brooke pointed to fans of light coming down the steps from the cottage. "The police are here."

But the police wouldn't reach the dock in time to stop the widow's rampage.

Judith jabbed Milton in the stomach with the cane, attempting to push him into the freezing water. He doubled over.

Faith rushed out from behind the boathouse. "Stop! It's over, Judith."

Those on the dock stared at Faith for a moment, probably as startled by seeing a woman in a vintage gown as by her sudden appearance.

"Judith, you're the one who followed me to town that night," Faith said, approaching them. "You stalked me in the garden maze and tried to peek in my windows."

"And you left a threatening note on my car," Brooke added.

Judith seemed surprised. But she recovered quickly and swung the cane full force at Faith's head.

Milton flung up an arm in front of her, deflecting the blow and saving Faith from Owen's fate. He grasped the cane with his other hand. He wrestled with Judith on the edge of the dock, their feet sliding on the slick boards.

Watson darted behind Judith. At the same instant, Boomer jumped up, his sturdy front paws landing solidly on Judith's thighs. She tumbled backward, flipping over Watson and off the dock.

For a moment, everyone froze in place, stunned.

Milton came to his senses first. He ran to the side of the boathouse and grabbed a red-and-white life preserver ring, then tossed it to Judith.

Faith scanned the dock for Watson, but she didn't see him.

While Milton and Brooke struggled to reach Judith, Faith knelt beside Owen. She had to lean past the hoopskirt spreading around her to grasp his arm. A lump had already risen on the side of his head, but he was breathing.

"Owen, it's Faith."

He moaned and opened his eyes.

"We've got to get you somewhere warm," she said. "Do you think you can stand?"

Owen grunted in reply.

Judith sputtered and gasped, complaining loudly as she was dragged from the water.

Milton pulled off his coat and wrapped it around the shivering woman.

Boomer paced around Milton, appearing ready to protect him from Judith.

Thudding footsteps shook the dock as Officers Bryan Laddy and Jan Rooney arrived. Wolfe followed, looking concerned.

"Thank you," Faith mouthed.

Wolfe nodded at her, then followed Glenn as he unlocked the boathouse and switched on the dock lights, driving away the darkness.

"I'll get the propane heater going," Glenn said. "You folks get inside and out of the weather."

Wolfe and Officer Laddy supported Owen, leading him to the boathouse. Milton assisted Agnes, and Officer Rooney escorted a soaking-wet Judith inside.

"Come on, Faith," Brooke said.

Faith still hadn't located her cat. She glanced around again. "Where's Watson?"

The women exchanged glances, then raced to the side of the dock where Judith had plunged into the icy water. If Glenn had not turned on the dock lights, they might not have seen him. Bobbing on the choppy waves, barely above the water, was a small black-and-white face.

Faith lunged forward, ready to save her cat.

But Brooke held her back. "You can't jump in. You'll get hypothermia."

The cat's head went underwater.

"Watson!"

Suddenly Boomer burst past Faith and Brooke. He leaped off the dock, landed in the water with a splash, and plunged under the waves.

For a moment, Faith feared they had lost both pets, but then Boomer popped back up. He held Watson by the scruff of the cat's neck.

Faith and Brooke lay flat on the dock, straining to reach the animals. Faith grabbed a very soggy Watson, and Brooke grappled to hang on to the short-haired dachshund.

Wolfe sprinted onto the dock, sliding to a halt beside the women. He joined Brooke in hoisting the slippery dog from the cold water. Then he helped Faith to her feet and ushered her and Brooke into the boathouse.

"Boomer!" Milton ran over to Brooke. He took Boomer from her arms, then clutched the shivering dog to his chest. "My poor puppy. How did you end up in the water?"

"He's a hero," Brooke said. "He went in after Watson."

Faith cradled the soaked cat to her chest, not thinking about the vintage blue gown that had made her feel like a princess earlier that evening. Now all that mattered was Watson. Was he breathing? Could a human perform CPR on a cat? She wished Midge was with them.

"What were you ladies doing?" Officer Rooney asked.

"Watson." Faith felt tears trail down her cheeks.

Glenn pushed two chairs close to the propane heater. Wolfe steered Faith to one of them, and Milton took the other seat while Boomer shivered in his lap.

"Let's get Watson and Boomer dried off," Brooke said. "Give them a rubdown to get the circulation going."

Glenn retrieved a few colorful beach towels and handed them to Faith and Milton.

As Faith dried Watson, patting the salty water from the cat's fur with the towel, she prayed fervently.

Milton and Brooke rubbed Boomer with beach towels until he was dry.

All the while, Boomer kept his somber brown eyes locked on Watson.

Faith studied her cat. "I think he's breathing."

"He's opening his eyes," Brooke said. "Hi, Watson."

When Faith felt a purr rumble in Watson's chest, she sobbed with relief and joy.

"Say now," Glenn said soothingly. "No need for tears. Your cat's gonna be okay."

"It's a good thing cats have nine lives," Officer Laddy said. "Because I'm pretty sure Watson used one up tonight."

22

Saturday became a whirlwind. First thing in the morning Faith drove to the police station to give her statement. The interview turned out to be as stressful as she'd expected. Faith tried to stick to the facts and not embellish with her own opinions.

Then she made an afternoon appointment with Midge's veterinarian clinic to check Watson for any ill effects from being dunked in the ocean and nearly drowned. If he received a clean bill of health, he would go to the pet spa at the manor to have his fur thoroughly cleaned.

She was in no rush to return the ruined vintage gown, but Charlotte called to invite her to the Jaxon family private quarters on the third floor for midmorning tea.

Charlotte might rightfully expect Faith to pay for restoring the gown or for replacing it with a replica. Neither option would be cheap. But the worst part would be seeing Charlotte's disappointment. Faith had been entrusted with a Jaxon family treasure, and she had destroyed it.

She stepped into the elevator, her heart thumping. The enormous dress box balanced in her arms seemed heavier than before. Probably from the mud and seawater soaking the once-gorgeous fabric.

Watson sat at her feet. Normally he didn't care for riding in the elevator, but today he seemed remarkably calm, even after his near-death experience. But his stiff, rumpled fur gave him a distressed look.

"You're as much of a disaster as the dress," Faith told the cat. "But at least your fur can be cleaned in the spa. I'm not sure this lovely gown can be saved."

When the elevator door opened, she was startled to see Wolfe. He took the box from Faith and led her and Watson to the informal living room, then set the dress box on the coffee table.

Charlotte smiled and motioned for Faith to take a seat next to her on the sofa. Charlotte's attire and hairstyle were much less formal than last night's, but she was still elegant in tailored pants and a lavender sweater.

Faith was glad she had dressed up more than she typically would have on a day off.

"You seem rested, Faith," Charlotte said, "although Watson isn't quite his usual debonair self."

As if to refute Charlotte's comment, Watson strutted around the coffee table. He wrapped himself around Charlotte's ankles and purred.

Charlotte reached down to rub his head.

"I'm taking him to Midge's clinic this afternoon," Faith said. "Then he's going to the spa. He'll be good as new."

"Thank goodness everyone is all right. When I think of what might have happened . . ." Charlotte's voice trailed off, and she shuddered.

Wolfe rested a hand on his mother's shoulder.

Faith turned to Wolfe. "You must have received my voice mail."

He nodded as he sat down in a chair. "The security guards alerted me when Judith and Milton left the banquet. When I saw that you had called me, I asked them to stop you, but it was too late. You and Brooke were already gone."

"Fortunately, Mr. Dobie noticed activity on the dock," Charlotte said. "He called the police."

"I have never driven so fast through the grounds," Wolfe added.

"We're just grateful Judith couldn't carry out her plan," Charlotte said. "She may return to her right mind one day and realize what a blessing it was that she was prevented from killing Mr. Waldrin."

"And Mr. Chase," Wolfe said. "It sounded like she intended to eliminate everyone associated with the *Essex* scrimshaw."

They chatted for a few more minutes, sipping tea and nibbling delicious mini scones, until the moment of truth arrived. Faith needed to leave for Midge's clinic soon. She couldn't put it off any longer.

"You've been very kind to me, but now I have to show you what I did to the dress." Faith lifted the lid and reached inside. The blue fabric didn't rustle like before. It felt limp. She pulled out the jewelry box and held it out to Charlotte. "Here's your ivory comb."

"The comb and the dress belong together," Charlotte said, accepting it with a smile. She turned it over in her hands, then laid it on the coffee table. "They're a perfect match."

"I am so sorry. I didn't stop to think when I grabbed Watson." Faith partially lifted the dress from the box. "There are water stains on the bodice and mud on the hem from walking down the steps to the boathouse."

"I'm just happy you and Watson survived," Charlotte assured Faith. "You are far more important than some old gown from the attic."

"Thank you, but please let me know if there's any way I can help to restore this beautiful dress," Faith said.

"You'd be surprised at the skill of our housekeeping staff," Charlotte replied airily. "The launderers have plenty of experience with vintage clothing, what with all the historical retreats we do. My repayment will be seeing you wear the dress at another Castleton event."

Another event? Charlotte expected Faith to dress up again? Faith was relieved but a little alarmed too. Her experience in the blue gown had been terrifying. Still, the thought of dressing like a princess again, with the ivory comb in her hair, did have a certain appeal.

"My mother may be gracious about the dress," Wolfe said, "but you owe me."

Faith's heart sank. She had disappointed her employer.

He smiled. "I didn't have the chance to claim the dance you promised me."

Faith was certain he was joking, attempting to lighten the conversation. But she felt blood rush to her cheeks in what was no doubt an obvious blush. "Thank you for being so understanding. If you'll please excuse me, Watson has his vet appointment."

They left the manor and drove to Midge's clinic. Midge examined Watson and pronounced the handsome tuxedo cat in excellent health. Then she rewarded him with some tunaroons.

After a trip to the pet spa to thoroughly clean the salt out of Watson's fur, cat and human finally returned home, where both collapsed into bed for much-needed rest.

By Sunday morning, the sun had returned, melting snow off the streets. Faith drove to Lighthouse Bay to attend church services with Eileen. She was determined to give proper thanks for Watson's survival.

Afterward, she and Eileen stopped at Snickerdoodles for coffee and pastries to go. Eileen offered to help Faith find Watson's escape route and prevent him from another disastrous adventure.

As soon as Faith opened the front door to the cottage, she sensed that Watson was gone.

"I have an idea where he went," Faith told her aunt. "Do you want to go for a drive or a walk?"

"It's so lovely today," Eileen said. "The sunshine seems to have calmed my arthritis and lifted my spirits after this stretch of gloomy weather. Let's walk."

They bundled up in case the breeze off the ocean was brisk, then set out at a leisurely pace, carrying their coffees and bag of pastries. In daylight, the scenery was breathtaking. The manor rose above dormant lawns and leafless trees, and Faith gloried in the golden beauty of late autumn.

They heard voices well before they reached the boathouse.

Standing at the end of the dock, Tasi held her Persian cat, Alika. Close beside her stood Milton and Boomer. Watson sat beside the dachshund, staring out to sea. Although Tasi was taller than Milton they looked like a matched set in gray coats. The humans gestured toward the ocean at something Faith could not see.

"Good morning," Faith called as she and Eileen approached the group. "I'm so glad you both extended your stays at the manor after all the unfortunate excitement we had this week."

"I didn't want to leave on a sour note," Tasi said. "Why should I be in a hurry to return to boring tropical weather when New England offers such variety?"

They all laughed.

"As a bonus," Milton said, "we have both been asked to evaluate the *Essex* scrimshaw."

"Expert witnesses," Tasi added. "Along with Owen."

"Is he going to be okay?" Eileen asked.

Milton nodded. "It was a concussion. He spent one night in the hospital, but he's already been released."

They chatted about the conference and the weather, and then in a somber turn, discussed Raymond's murder at the hands of his wife.

"What about Agnes?" Faith asked.

"The police handed over the *Essex* scrimshaw to her," Milton replied, "and she'll be overseeing the family estate. The rest of the collection was found hidden in Judith's room. No one had stolen the other pieces after all."

Eileen held out the bag from Snickerdoodles. "I'm afraid we don't have coffee for everyone, but we have pastries to share."

Tasi shivered as she took a pastry from the bag. "The weather is not entirely suitable for a picnic on the dock."

"We should go back to the manor," Eileen suggested.

"We've waited this long. Let's hold out for a few more minutes." Milton turned his attention to the ocean.

"What are you looking for?" Faith asked.

"Whales," Tasi and Milton said at the same time.

"Whale watching is a tourist attraction here as well as at my home in Hawaii," Tasi said. "Typically, the whales are much farther offshore, but we decided to take our chances at seeing one today."

As they waited, Faith touched Milton's arm. "Your dog saved Watson's life. I can't tell you what that means to me. If there's ever anything I can do for you and Boomer, please let me know."

Milton gave her a shy smile. "Watson's been good for him. Really helped him come out of his shell."

"And probably his kennel," Faith quipped.

They all laughed again.

Watson meowed softly.

Faith studied her cat, impeccably groomed after his trip to the pet spa. Watson had been here when Boomer dug up the harpoon and *Essex* scrimshaw. He had nearly lost his life on this very dock Friday night. And here he was again, despite the dangers he had faced. Had whale watching been what drew him to the dock repeatedly?

Whatever had brought him here, he and Boomer had helped to capture a killer.

Watson meowed, louder this time. He stood.

"I see one," Tasi announced.

"Where?" Eileen asked. "I don't see anything."

"That way," Tasi said, pointing.

Eileen gasped. "Oh my! Now I see them."

Faith strained to see across the calm water. In the distance, she noticed a curve of gray crest the surface of the ocean. Then another one.

Watson and Boomer stood side by side. If they had been humans, Faith could imagine one throwing a brotherly arm across the other's shoulders.

The group watched in silence for several minutes until the whales moved farther out to sea and out of sight.

Milton picked up Boomer and carried him along the dock toward the stairs.

Faith lifted Watson in her arms. A purr rumbled in his chest. As she turned, Watson and Tasi's cat touched noses briefly.

"Our pets really bonded," Faith said. "Watson is really going to miss Boomer and Alika."

Milton and Tasi exchanged shy smiles.

"We'll be back next year," Milton said.

"We've both been invited to speak at the next New England Whaling in History and Literature Conference," Tasi explained.

"Which will be held at Castleton Manor again," Milton reminded them.

"We love it here," Tasi said.

Faith wasn't sure whether the "we" meant Tasi and her cat or Tasi and Milton.

Either way, Faith had to agree. She couldn't imagine living anywhere else.